To Aaron, Amber, and Shanda for strengthening my sense of purpose.

Contents

Chapter One

The Beginning

Austin Martin Annenkeng was born on October 20, 1976, in Mbengwi, Cameroon. Mbengwi is a small rural town located in the English-speaking Northwest Region of Cameroon. The town is famous in the region for its chronic stillness, as not much has changed in it for more than half a century. Consequently, every ambitious person who grows up there eventually leaves in search of better opportunities in other Cameroonian towns and cities or out of the country. This practice, commonly known in Cameroon as rural exodus, often leads to another very popular phenomenon called *brain flight*. The latter refers to the process of highly skilled, highly educated, and exceptionally talented young men and women being compelled by widespread misery, epidemics, rampant death, epic systemic corruption, and extremely limited career opportunities in Cameroon to seek greener pastures abroad, even in some of the most hostile and incredibly immigrant-unfriendly countries on the planet. It is not uncommon for scores of Cameroonians to perish annually while trying to flee the hardship in their country. For a highly indebted third-world country struggling desperately to come out of poverty, it is pathetically ironic to say that its own finest brains, which could build and save it, are making significant contributions to the development and economies of other countries that have welcomed them.

Austin was the third of eight children born to Robert and Juliette Annenkeng. His older brother, Robert Jr., passed away a couple of weeks after birth, thereby making Austin the first living son and transferring all the responsibilities that rest on the shoulders of the first son in an African family to him. He had an older sister, Julia. His parents were devout Catholics who instilled profound Christian values into their children from birth and ensured that their offspring upheld these values their entire lives.

Robert got married to Juliette right out of high school in 1965 through prearranged marriage, which was very common at the time. They both hailed from Dchang, a city in the French-speaking West Region of Cameroon. Upon graduating from high school with a technical diploma in plumbing, Robert was hired by the government of Cameroon and assigned to the Ministry of Mines and Power in Mbengwi, where his major tasks included the construction of a dam on the River Abi to generate hydroelectricity and the development of a water-pumping system to distribute water to households in the town. The former project was more than 60 percent completed when it was suspended by the government. It has never been completed even though there is an acute shortage of energy to power homes in the country. Electric power is so scarce nationwide that cities have to take turns going for days and even weeks without it. That's Cameroon.

After further training, in 1985 Robert joined the national water corporation, known by its French acronym SNEC, where he was an exemplary employee until his retirement in 2003. He received several medals and awards in recognition of his hard work and dedication to the company.

For her part, Juliette, on arrival in Mbengwi in the late sixties, opened a small convenience store. She noticed that there was also a demand for cooked food, since the store was located across the road from the town's only clinic and the regional office of internal revenue. Consequently, she started selling food that she personally cooked. An eating area was set up in the store to serve hungry customers, whose numbers increased daily.

One day a patron asked for a bottle of beer with his lunch. He was shocked when he was told that the business did not sell alcohol. He asked what kind of restaurant did not sell beer. Cameroonians like a nice cold bottle of beer or wine with their lunch and dinner. At the incessant request of her customers, Juliette started selling alcohol without a license and continued for several years until she eventually decided to make it another legitimate part of her business.

Additional space was needed to accommodate this. She worked very hard every day of the week to keep the business open and to be a great wife and mother. She took her children to work, and Robert would join her there and help out when he got off his own work. The family probably spent more time at the business place than at home. In fact, as soon as the kids were able to count, they were helping there in one way or another. This is not child labor or abuse. It is standard practice in families that own small or large businesses in Cameroon. Due to strong traditional, cultural, and family values, children could be around alcohol, cigarettes, and other age-inappropriate items at the family business without ever harboring the thought of trying them. Juliette and her husband inculcated these values in their children very early, along with a deep work ethic, honesty, integrity, and resilience.

In 1970, a few years after arriving in Mbengwi, Robert and Juliette bought a piece of land that was not far from the business and started building a small mud house, but they were abruptly forced to cease construction before the house could be completed. Six months into the project, she almost lost her life in a ghastly car accident on her way to buy supplies to replenish the store. She was traveling to Bamenda, a city located about twenty-five miles from Mbengwi, when the public-transportation vehicle she was riding in skidded off the dirt road and rolled over several times down a valley before resting on its roof against a mango tree.

The driver and three other passengers were killed in the accident, and Juliette sustained several life-threatening injuries and spent two months in the hospital. She still bears huge scars from that accident. The medical bills drained their finances to the point where they had to move out of the house they were renting into their partially finished house. They hoped to eventually get back on their feet and finish constructing the house. Unfortunately, they were never able to entirely finish the house, due to their growing family, education costs for their children, illnesses, business burglaries, and some unwise financial decisions.

It was in the midst of all these struggles that Austin was born. His parents had waited impatiently for his birth for two reasons. They were extremely excited to be expecting another baby, as less than twenty-four months earlier, they had lost their first male child just a couple of weeks after his birth. Additionally, they were eager to know the gender of the new baby. Juliette desperately wanted to give Robert a boy, since the first child was a girl, and, in the traditional Bamileke society from which they hailed, a wife is expected to give her husband a male child, a successor to continue the lineage and heritage.

Thus, it was with tremendous elation that Austin's parents welcomed him into the world on October 20, 1976, at 9:15 a.m. He weighed a little over nine pounds and was a carbon copy of his father. He had his father's large nose, thick lips, and brown eyes. His front hairline above his forehead was perfectly M-shaped, like Robert's. In addition, Austin had flat feet, and his toes and fingers were just like his father's: huge.

Out of an abundance of caution, Robert and Juliette decided to stay in the hospital with Austin even after they were discharged, just to make sure the doctors ran enough tests and checked, observed, and monitored the baby long enough to make sure that he did not have any diseases, especially the mysterious condition that had killed Robert Jr. almost two years earlier. Witnesses said that Junior's urine was white-like milk and that he cried for hours without stopping, as if he was in excruciating pain.

Nevertheless, Junior's illness and his death were never discussed in the family. In fact, Austin and his five younger siblings did not even know that they had an older brother who had passed away. An uncle mentioned the subject to Austin in passing one day when he was about seventeen.

"You look just like Joseph," he said.

"Who's Joseph?" Austin asked.

"He was your big brother. He died two weeks after he was born. Papa and Mami haven't told you about him?"

"No."

"Maybe they'll tell you when they're ready, or perhaps they don't want you to be depressed about it."

Austin wondered why his parents never mentioned his older brother. He suspected it must have been a very painful subject, and he resolved never to ask them or to ever mention it to his siblings. But he secretly imagined what his life would have been like if his brother had not died.

Seventeen days after he was born, Austin's parents took him home. He had outlived his late brother by three days, and the doctors and nurses reassured them that he was in perfect health. The happy parents made sure that the baby got all his needed immunizations and remembered to take him back to the hospital for his monthly checkups until he was one year old. On the day the newborn was taken home, Robert's colleagues, neighbors, friends, and family members who had traveled from other parts of Cameroon gathered at the Annenkengs' to celebrate his birth.

The baby quickly grew into a toddler. He was walking effortlessly at one, speaking pretty clearly at two, and demanding to go to school at three. No school would accept him at that age. Kids were allowed into nursery school or kindergarten at four and into class one, or first grade, at six. However, Austin skipped the former, and an exception was made to allow him into the latter at age five.

Chapter Two

Primary School

At the age of five, Austin was enrolled in the first grade at Government School (GS), Mbengwi. He was so excited on the eve of his first day of school. That night, he slept in his parents' bed because he wanted them to wake him up early to get ready for school. At about 2:15 a.m., he woke up with a start and screamed, "Mami! Papa! It's daybreak! I heard the cock crowing! I need to get ready for school. I don't want to be late!" The crowing of the cock very often signaled the dawn of the day, as the chicken that the family was raising would start crowing around five o'clock every morning. Unfortunately for Austin, the crow he heard that morning was a false alarm given by a rooster that might have lost its sense of time, was suffering from a sleep disorder, or, like the impatient soon-to-be first-grader, was just eager to get its day started.

He did not return to sleep that night. When his father woke up at 5:00 a.m. to get ready for work, he gave the five-year-old a bath and put on his school uniform, which consisted of a blue short-sleeve button-down shirt, khaki shorts, and all-white canvas shoes. His mother made breakfast, which included a sandwich, an omelet, and a cup of tea for both "men of the house," as she fondly referred to them. She carried Austin's three-year-old sister, Judith, on her back while making breakfast, as the toddler would not let her parents get out of the bed without her. Usually she would not even notice them getting out of bed, but that morning was different. Her brother's excitement about school could be felt in his singing and humming of "One two three four five, can you catch a fish alive."

At 6:30 a.m., Austin's father walked him to GS Mbengwi. The school was a forty-eight-minute walk from their home, but for the eager boy, it felt like half a day. When they finally made it to the school, they looked around for his classroom, class one. They had been looking for a couple of minutes when he suddenly screamed, "I found it! That sign says class one!"

His teacher, Ms. Forbang, was walking into her classroom right at that instant, and she turned around to see who the seemingly enthusiastic pupil was. "Oh wow!" she exclaimed. "Who's this very clean and smart young man?"

"My name is Austin Martin Annenkeng. I am five years old. This is my father. His name is Robert Kemdong Annenkeng, and my mother's name is Juliette Matango Annenkeng. Are you going to be my please madam?"

He had heard the expression "please madam" from some kids in his neighborhood, and he suspected it must have been an advanced term for teacher. For a kid who wanted to leave a splashing and memorable first impression on his teacher and peers on first contact, he hit the nail right on the head, as Ms. Forbang immediately understood that she had in front of her a smart, talkative, and inquisitive kid who was not even old enough to be in class one.

"Yes, I'll be your please madam, your teacher. I am so happy to have you in my class."

Austin hit the ground running the first day of school. He worked very hard in class and asked questions about everything, including things he understood, just to make sure, and also to gain the attention of his peers. He made sure that he did his homework every evening and would attempt to teach his parents the alphabet; colors; the numbers one through one hundred; the provinces, divisions, and cities in Cameroon; and simple addition and subtraction. One evening toward the end of the first term, he told his parents he no longer wanted to become a plumber like dad. He wanted to be a teacher one day, like Ms. Forbang, to teach people things. He flew through class one with ease, and the following year, he was in class two.

Austin found class two a lot easier than the preceding grade level, but that did not make him complacent. In fact, his assiduity, inquisitiveness, and passion for learning increased. He told his parents he did not need help getting up or getting ready for school in the morning. He would get ready for school daily at 6:00 a.m., right when his father would be preparing for work. After breakfast, the two of them would embark on the forty-eight-minute walk to GS Mbengwi. Their conversation on the way usually centered on Austin's schoolwork from the previous day, any homework he might have had, and what he expected to learn on the new day.

In class he sat right in the first row. He had a male teacher, Mr. Tah, who would whip the kids for any misbehavior. One day, a classmate stole Austin's arithmetic homework, and he got a whipping when the teacher checked every student's work and noticed that Austin didn't have his. He swore to his teacher that his parents had helped him with the homework all night and that his father had even double-checked his work on the way to school that morning, but Mr. Tah would not take any excuses. "No homework equals six strikes. Full stop!" the bald fifty-five-year-old instructor yelled sternly. Austin started crying before the strokes began landing on his little palms. The pain traveled to all parts of his body and paralyzed him all day.

After school was dismissed, he walked home, as he always did, with other kids who lived in his neighborhood. When he arrived at his mom's business premises, she immediately noticed the he was not his usual energetic and excited self. He told her then and later his father what had happened in class. They both promised to speak to his teacher first thing in the morning.

The next day, Austin's father calmly explained to Mr. Tah that he had helped his son with the homework and that he had double-checked the work before they got to school. "If Austin did not have his notebook, it must have been stolen in your classroom by one of your students," Mr. Annenkeng said. Then he added, "I suggest you have a notebook check in class today to find out who has my son's book. He worked too hard on that assignment to not get a grade for it."

The teacher asked Austin and his father to describe the missing note-book. He also took the angry young man's English notebook to get a sample of his handwriting.

When class started, Mr. Tah decided to go around, unannounced, and check everybody's arithmetic exercise book. Three desks behind Austin sat a notorious student named Joseph. He got a whipping every day for coming late, disrupting class, sleeping in class, fighting, or steal-ing from classmates. He was trying to hide something hurriedly under his desk when the teacher leaped in his direction and yelled, "Don't even try! Let me see that notebook!"

Mr. Tah seized the notebook, and before he could even ask, Austin screamed with palpable astonishment, "That's my exercise book!" The culprit had extracted the arithmetic notebook out of Austin's book bag the previous morning when he was busy helping another classmate complete the homework before it was checked.

Mr. Tah was livid, especially since the thief had erased Austin's name and written his on the book and was trying desperately to prove that it was his, even though the handwriting on all the classwork and assign-ments was clearly Austin's. The teacher did exactly what teachers at the school did to students like Joseph. He grabbed his paddle and gave the rascal ten licks. The teacher also apologized to Austin and made Joseph do the same.

The rest of that school year went on hitch free for Austin. He made a couple of new friends, Christian and Stanley. They collaborated in class, played soccer together during breaks, and shared their lunches. Austin was usually the mouthpiece for his friends, who were very shy. They kept quiet in class, even when they knew the answers to questions asked by the teacher. At the end of that academic year, the three friends easily got promoted to the third grade.

When school got out for the summer that year, Austin's parents al-lowed him some extra privileges as a result of his excellent grades. He was allowed to visit Stanley and Christian and even spent the night at their homes, with the permission of their parents. He also earned the privilege of hanging out even longer with the neighbors' children. The kids in his neighborhood usually spent several hours daily playing soccer and table tennis and crafting toy cars, guns, airplanes, tractors, miniature houses, chairs, tables, and benches out of materials such as bamboo, Styrofoam, wood, empty boxes, and empty cans.

Their parents, who spent eight to twelve hours daily working on their farms, barely made enough money to put a decent dinner on the table or afford the shirts on their backs. Their clothes and shoes were the old, unwanted outfits of well-to-do individuals in the community. Therefore, these kids never got a toy for Christmas or birthdays. They wore the same clothes every day and would wash them on Saturday to wear to church on Sunday. Sometimes they would sell the toys they crafted to buy treats they hardly ever tasted, such as candy and ice cream.

Apart from enhancing his soccer and table tennis skills and learning how to craft homemade toys, Austin also acquired some bad behaviors from the mostly self-supervising neighborhood boys and girls that summer. For instance, he started telling lies to his parents, first over less significant things, such as whether he had washed his hands before eating or whether he had brushed his teeth before going to bed. But, progressively, his lies started involving more important things, such as his daily assigned reading and arithmetic assignments and feeding the chickens and pigs.

One day that summer, he returned home at about 5:00 p.m. after playing soccer for a couple of hours with his neighborhood friends. Habitually, he would bathe before the family met at the dinner table for the evening meal, but that evening he simply soaked a towel and wiped his feet, hands, arms, and face; applied body lotion to these parts; and changed his clothes. Before he could finish this fraud, his mother called, "Austin! It's dinnertime."

"I'll be right there," he said.

A minute later, he was at the table with the rest of the family, sitting right next to his father, to the latter's right hand. Grace was said by Julia,

Austin's older sister. When she finished, she whispered in her mother's ear, "Mom, do you smell that? Somebody smells musty and sweaty!"

It was not difficult to identify the source of the smell. Everybody knew Austin had been playing soccer that evening, so his father asked, "Austin, did you take a bath before coming to dinner?"

He answered confidently and with a straight face, "Yes!"

But all his father had to do was lean slightly to his right to smell the evidence to the contrary. His parents were very angry and disappointed that he had lied. He was allowed to finish his dinner, but as soon as he swallowed the last piece of fish, he was summarily dismissed to bathe thoroughly and report to his mother for verification before going to bed. As punishment for lying, he was not allowed to play with his friends for the next two days. He had to spend that time doing something productive, including reading and summarizing every chapter of *The White Man of God*, by Kenjo Jumbam; feeding the goats, pigs, and chickens; mopping the floors; and sweeping the yard.

Apart from the habit of dissembling, Austin started learning about male and female relationships and gossiping from his buddies. For example, he learned from Freddie that a married man is a husband, while a married woman is a wife. Prior to that valuable lesson, Austin referred to the former as the father and the latter as the mother. For instance, earlier that summer, his mother had sent him to give a can of milk to her friend, Mrs. Kisob, who lived a couple of houses away. Moments later, Austin returned to tell his mother that the lady was not at home and that he had given the milk to her father.

"She didn't tell me that her father would be visiting," his mom said. "Are you sure it was her father?"

"Yes, I see him there all the time. He said I should tell Papa thanks for letting him use the wheelbarrow and that he will return it tomorrow," said Austin.

That was when his mother realized that he was calling her friend's husband her father, but she didn't correct him.

Kids back then were very shy and scared to let their parents know that they were aware of male and female relationships, as that implied that they were conscious of an even greater taboo: sexual relationships and intercourse. Therefore, children would use the most innocent of terms to appear ignorant of these things, even if they were not ignorant of them. It was just safer for them, because most parents would whip the crap out of their child if they realized that he or she knew about male and female relationships—or much worse, if they were sex-conscious. Austin learned all of these things from his friends that summer, and it would lead him into major trouble at school and at home the following fall.

Chapter Three

A Rude Awakening

School resumed on September 9, 1983, and, unlike the two previous academic years, it was a changed Austin who showed up to Mr. Ofuka's third-grade class at GS Mbengwi. He had become extremely playful and disruptive. Additionally, as seen earlier, he was becoming more and more fond of girls and less and less likely to tell the truth about things. He no longer wanted to sit in front, as he had done in grades one and two. At his request, he was assigned a seat in the last row of the fifth column, the column farthest from the teacher's desk. His friends, Christian and Stanley, joined him there.

It did not take long for the teacher to discover that Austin was very bad news. He hardly participated in class activities. His constant talking, laughing, and playing hindered effective teaching and learning from occurring almost on a daily basis. He was no longer scared of the whipping that misbehaving students usually received. As a result, his teacher had to try other things, such as changing his seat, taking points from his grade, making him stand in a corner of the classroom, and making him pick a pin (a punishment consisting of bending forward and touching the floor with the right index finger while simultaneously raising the right leg in the air for periods ranging from twenty minutes to one hour, depending on the severity of the offense). None of these worked. Consequently, Mr. Ofuka started kicking Austin out of his classroom whenever he misbehaved. That meant he would miss the classwork and assignments.

Austin's misbehavior greatly affected his grades. When he got his report card at the end of the first term, right before Christmas, he saw that he had failed every subject, including his favorite one, English. He had the lowest average in every subject. His teachers made some blistering comments on the report card, such as "Austin is the class clown. He does not care about learning. He is not afraid of the consequences of misbehaving. He will keep failing if he does not change." Surprisingly, Austin was shocked by the grades and the comments, as if he was not expecting them.

How was he going to explain this to his parents? They were going to skin him alive! For the first time that year, he was scared and miserable. He froze when he asked to see his friends' report cards. Both of them had passed, barely. They started laughing at him and teasing him. Stanley said, "Chris, guess who's not getting a Christmas present this year!"

"That would be Mr. Austin over here. Ha-ha!" said Christian and added, "I think someone is going to pee in his pants today when he gets a nice flogging. That would be fun to watch. Stanlo, would you like to go see?"

That made Austin furious, and he clenched his fists and swung viciously, missing Christian's right eye by less than an inch. Having obtained their schadenfreude, the two sadistic friends took off running, leaving behind Austin, who had a lot of thinking to do. He had to come up with a strategy to break the terrible news to his parents.

Austin loitered on campus for over two hours after dismissal to brood about his parents' reaction to his dramatic failure. He thought about his successes in the first and second grades and how proud his mother and father had been at the end of each term when he brought home his report card with grades that would have made Archimedes envious. If he could just turn the clock back to eight months prior, he would be going home to praise, presents, and prospects of a promising future, but, alas, that wasn't possible. He thought about going home and telling his parents that his teacher had lost his report card but quickly gave up that foolish idea. "Mom and Dad will find out where my teacher lives and get the truth from him. That will make matters worse!" he told himself. He also considered changing the failing grades to passing ones. He sat in the shade of some trees on the side of the road to explore this solution in detail, but it didn't take him long to realize the major challenges that strategy was fraught with. All the passing grades were handwritten in blue ink, while all the failing grades and negative remarks were in red. Therefore, it looked as if someone had bled all over his report card. "Even if I could figure out a way to change these grades, I don't have a blue pen. Even my younger sister, Judith, would be able to identify my handwriting on Mr. Ofuka's handwriting," he thought. "Oh Papa God, I am screwed!" he screamed. Anybody within a hundred yards might have heard his scream. Finally, he said a prayer and resigned himself to whatever fate awaited him at home. He stood up and continued on his way.

Austin made it home that evening a little bit after six thirty. His family was already gathered at the table for dinner, but they were not going to start eating without him. There was someone else at the table too. His uncle Joseph was visiting from Yaoundé. He was Austin's favorite uncle, because he always brought presents. In addition, each time he visited, he would take his nephew and nieces for a walk, and they would stop somewhere to get cold sodas, cookies, and candy. He was also very protective of the little ones. He would not let their parents, Austin's mom and dad, raise their voices at them or put their hands on them in his presence. Austin wished he were around often, but Joseph's job and family kept him very busy. He was a truck driver who spent his free time as the manager at a casino.

That evening, Joseph was the first to see Austin when he arrived extremely late from school. He was sitting at the end of the table facing the door; hence, he had a full view of everybody at the table and everything outside the door as far as the eye could see.

"Austin! How was school?" Joseph screamed with gusto when the failure appeared at the door, opposite him.

"I flunked," Austin said, just loud enough for anybody who was listening closely.

His mother gasped. Austin stood at the door and would not cross the threshold. He didn't budge when his father told him to bring the report card, for he was afraid of what he might do to him. He dropped the report card on the floor and started retreating when his father stood up and started walking toward him to get the report card.

"Did he really fail?" his mother asked.

"Yes! Terribly too, unless this is some other kid's report card," his father said with conspicuous shock.

He returned to the table and sat down quietly. The silence at the table was palpable for about five minutes. And then, suspecting what was going to befall Austin, Uncle Joseph left the table to get Austin. He had his protégé sit very close to him and gave a speech to his parents about failure—how success wouldn't be sweet enough without moments of weaknesses and setbacks. "Even Albert Einstein and Isaac Newton failed miserably in their early school years before rising to monumental success later on in life. Leave the child alone, and help him learn from his mistakes," the uncle said.

As he continued speaking, the tension at the table eased progressively, and everybody started eating. The anxiety and fear in Austin also dissipated slightly, although he still couldn't summon enough appetite to enjoy the spaghetti and beef dinner, his favorite meal. His mother had cooked it in anticipation of Austin's and Julia's excellent report cards.

The rest of dinner was slightly jovial. The adults talked about Uncle Joseph's jobs, his wife and daughter, how long he was visiting, Austin's mother's business, politics, and sports. After the meal, Julia helped her mother clear the table, and at eight thirty, her brother and she were dismissed to go to bed. Austin walked to his room like an inmate walking to the electric chair. Even though his parents had not done or said anything to him, he knew he was not out of danger yet. He was certain it was just the clam before the storm. "They'll teach me a lesson after Uncle Joe leaves," he thought.

Uncle Joseph left two days later, on the morning of December 22. Austin's father did not go to work on that day. His mother was not in a hurry to go to her business premises either. The entire family walked their guest to the side of the main road at Mile 17, where they waited for a bus to pick him up. After waiting for about thirty-seven minutes, the visitor was picked up by an overloaded bus for the one-hour journey to Bamenda, where he would take another bus bound for Yaoundé.

On the way back to the house, Austin's father brought up the problem of the report card for the first time in forty-eight hours. He asked what had happened for the phenomenally smart and enthusiastic boy to go from crème de la crème to the last student in the class in less than four months.

His mother did not give him a chance to answer the question. She immediately blamed everything on Austin's friends and all the time he had been spending with them since May that year.

"Since you started hanging out with Christian, Stanley, Mary, Edmond, Anthony, Evans, and the rest of the kids in this neighborhood, you haven't been the same. You've learned to tell lies, and now you can't even perform at average in any of your subjects. Well, I'll tell you what: you're going to get your act together, whether you like it or not."

She went on to inform Austin of the consequences of his actions. "Your father and I have decided that you'll not be spending one more second with those so-called friends. As of today, you'll have only three items on your daily schedule: house chores, school, and study or homework. I also need to see you read the Bible and pray at least twice daily. I don't need you helping me at the store anymore until I'm satisfied with your grades. Do you understand?"

"Yes, Mami," he said.

"You'll not be getting those blue-and-white Adidas tennis shoes you wanted for Christmas," his father added. "But if you're able to rise from the bottom to the top of your class by the end of the second term, I'll buy them for you, and your mother and I might consider reinstating some of your privileges."

He gave Austin a hug and reassured him that he had confidence that he could pull up his grades with consistent hard work and resilience.

Austin promised to just that. He could not believe what had just happened. Contrary to his expectations, all hell had not broken loose. His parents had given him a hug when he had expected them to flog his skin off. He heaved a sigh of relief and said a silent thank-you prayer to God. He was content with the sanctions that his parents had announced, for they were far less than what he had expected. He was determined to make them proud of him again.

That Christmas break was the longest ever to Austin, as he spent most of the time indoors studying while every other kid he knew was having fun. However, he sucked it up and waited patiently for school to resume on January 3. His father accidentally ran into his teacher at the city market on New Year's Eve. The teacher did not hesitate to complain about Austin's behavior and grades. Embarrassed, the parent promised the teacher that the student would apologize when school resumed and that everything would be done on the home front to ensure that the conduct from the first term would not continue into the second term.

As promised, on January 3, 1984, Austin's father got him to apologize for giving his teacher hell for the whole of the first term. For his part, the father said he was sorry for trusting that Austin was going to maintain the excitement, enthusiasm, and exemplary behavior from grades one and two. The apologies were matched with action, as Austin found his old self again, and his parents requested weekly updates from his teacher.

Austin steered his boat out of harm's way the rest of that school year. He remained friends with Christian and Stanley, but he didn't hang out with them as often as he did before. As far as his other friends in the neighborhood were concerned, his parents didn't allow him to spend time with them. He passed all his subjects during the second term and was fifth in order of merit when second-term reports went home. His success was remarkable the third and final term. He was top of the class and received an award for most improved student. He was on his way to class four.

He sailed through the fourth grade smoothly. Even if he wanted to fool around a little bit, he could not, because his new teacher, Mrs. Fomin, knew his mother very well, as they were from the same tribe. Austin found a new friend in his teacher's nephew, Anton. He also thought that Mrs. Fomin's daughter, Eunice, was gorgeous, even though she was two grades ahead of him. He liked it when she stopped by her mother's classroom daily before going to her classroom, during lunch break, and right after dismissal. He never could gather enough courage to approach her, much less get within seven feet of her. He would look at her pretty face and imagine having her as what his neighborhood friends had taught him—his girlfriend.

He started cooking up a plan to tell her exactly how he felt about her. "That's right! When I see her playing with her friends during break, I'll just walk up to her and tell her that she's very beautiful and that I want to be her boyfriend," he resolved.

He did not have to wait too long to meet Eunice. A few minutes after school got out the next day, he was talking to Mrs. Fomin about an assignment he didn't understand when Eunice walked in. She looked phenomenally beautiful, as usual.

"Did you have a good day in class today, honey?" her mother asked.

"Yes, Mommy! I got an A in arithmetic."

"Awesome! Did you greet Austin? Have you met him?"

"No, I've never met him, but he must be the Austin Anton talks about all the time. Hi, Austin!"

Austin froze. His heart was racing and pounding particularly loud. For several months he had longed for an opportunity to be in this girl's presence. He had even prayed for a chance to speak to her. There she was, less than a foot from him and speaking to him, but he could not even remember how to respond to a simple greeting.

On his way home that afternoon, all he could think about was how he had blown a golden opportunity to make an outstanding first impression on the girl of his dreams. There were only three weeks left in the school year. After that, he might not be able to see her again. He had to act fast. He was going to continue pursuing a great opportunity to speak to Eunice. That didn't come until six months later, when he was in the fifth grade.

Austin's fifth-grade year was very eventful. Academically, he was outstanding. Ms. Forbang, his first-grade teacher, was his teacher once again, and he liked her. She had inspired him to want to be a teacher like her in the future. He was consistently assiduous the entire school year, but he managed to find time to dedicate to his social life, starting the Eunice file.

Instead of looking for an opportunity to talk to her as he had previously decided, Austin made up his mind to write a love letter and have one of his friends deliver it to her. However, he had no idea how to write a love letter, even though facility with language was not one of his weaknesses. He found a solution to his problem one Thursday when he was paging through his sister's tenth-grade English textbook and came across a letter that a boy had written to a girl he was in love with. All he had to do was substitute the girl's name with Eunice's and the boy's name with his. When he was done working on the letter, it read thus:

> Dear Gorgeous Eunice,
> How are you? I just wanted to tell you that you are phenomenally pretty. You just look impressively outstanding. You have "fine" written all over you like an overdue library book. Each time I see you, I am mesmerized by your lavish beauty, and the great love I have for you jumps one level higher. I would be thrilled if I had the opportunity to have you as my girlfriend.
> Sincerely,
> Your wanting-to-be-boyfriend, Austin

He folded the finished product neatly and kept it in his pocket with the objective of having it delivered the next day. During lunch break the next day, he gave the letter to Christian to deliver it, but when the latter looked around the campus and found Eunice playing dodgeball with her friend, he panicked and shyly retreated without drawing attention to himself. Austin replaced the mail in his pocket and hoped to deliver it on Monday, but something really embarrassing happened that evening when he returned home.

One of his older sister's chores was to do the laundry for all the children. She preferred to do this on Friday evenings and forget about it. On this particular Friday, she got help from Didier, a cousin who had come to spend the weekend with Austin's family. Before they started handwashing the school uniforms, Didier decided to search the pockets just in case there was something important in any of them. He stumbled upon something carefully folded in Austin's back pocket. It was addressed to "My Dear Eunice." He asked Julia who Eunice was, but she didn't know her. Out of curiosity, he unfolded the letter and read it loudly, both of them laughing uncontrollably after each sentence. When he finished, Julia thought she had found a golden opportunity to make her brother pay for being so annoying toward her over several months.

At the dinner table that evening, everybody was excitedly talking about the week that had just ended. Papa talked about projects he had been able to complete at work, and Mami mentioned that the slowing economy was affecting her business. Julia talked about her good grades at school and how she wished she could finish high school a couple of years early to get away from her annoying brother.

Then came Austin's turn to give an account of his week, but before he could begin, Didier said, "Dear Gorgeous Eunice..." and Julia said, "You just look impressively outstanding." The parents looked very confused and asked the kids what was going on. They ignored the question, and Didier went further. "You have 'fine' written all over you like an overdue library book."

Julia and Didier were looking at Austin, who looked as if he had seen a ghost. It dawned on him that he had forgotten to retrieve his love letter to Eunice from his back pocket before giving up his school uniform for washing. He started trembling, as he didn't want his parents to find out he was writing love letters to girls. He excused himself to use the restroom, and Julia followed him.

Down the hallway, she whispered to him, "If you don't want me to tell Mom and Dad about the letter, you have to pay me. What's your offer?" Austin promised to give her his slice of meat at every meal for a whole week, but she declined. It was not worth the secret.

She was returning to the table to spill the beans when Austin pleaded desperately, almost loud enough to be heard at the table, "OK! Two weeks!" She was a couple of feet from the table when she told him one month or no deal. He agreed.

Back at the dinner table, Austin's dad asked what was going on one more time, and Julia said they were just reciting the lines from a new poem she had learned in school. It was her favorite poem, and she had been teaching Didier the poem while they were doing laundry. The lie was perfect, and Austin paid up. In fact, he passed his entire plate of rice and beef stew to Julia, who split it with the other schemer. Austin was not hungry anymore. He was just happy to have dodged a bullet. That episode shook him so badly that he gave up the idea of pursuing Eunice entirely. He would dedicate all his time to his education. Consequently, he easily earned his promotion to the next grade.

Austin knew that the sixth grade was the most important one, because, though not the final primary-school grade, he could take the government Common Entrance Examination in the sixth grade and skip grade seven. He had the full support of his parents, siblings, uncles, aunts, and close friends. They encouraged him to graduate early. Consequently, he started preparing in the summer after class five. He created a daily schedule to help him stay focused:

7:30 a.m.–9:30 a.m.: Wake up, brush teeth, eat breakfast, and do chores (clean my room and living room)
9:30 a.m.–1:30 p.m.: Study/read a book
1:30 p.m.–4:00 p.m.: Lunch break; play soccer or Ping-Pong or both
4:30 p.m.: Take a bath
5:30 p.m.–7:00 p.m.: Help mom at the store

7:15 p.m.: Eat dinner

8:10 p.m.–9:10 p.m.: Read a book and go to sleep

Church on Sunday followed by family time and light studying/reading

He followed the schedule with mathematical exactitude every day that summer.

Chapter Four

First Impressions Last a Lifetime

Austin had just concluded his study session one afternoon when he noticed two gray Volkswagen buses parked right in front of his home. It was not unusual for all kinds of cars, motorcycles, and bicycles to park there year-round, as the house sat right in front of the world-famous Abbi Falls. Tourists from all around Cameroon and the world would come daily to see the falls, the rock formation, the deep valley, and the uniquely beautiful flowers that grew therein. The plants surrounding the falls would not grow anywhere else in the world.

The individuals, all of them white, from Germany, Denmark, Sweden, Norway, Finland, Netherlands, Italy, France, the United States, England, and Canada, who had parked in front of Austin's home that afternoon, needed a native, preferably an adult, to take them down the falls to show them around. But all the adults were either at work or on their farms on that day. Even though he had not yet eaten his lunch, Austin volunteered to guide them the best he could down the valley. He suspected that these tourists were like the others he had met in the past, and if that was the case, they would be carrying food, and they might give him some for his service. He had been down there more than a hundred times and could maneuver the area even with his eyes closed.

After putting on more comfortable gear, he led the group of twenty-two tourists down the valley for a three-hour tour to see all the attractions. About an hour into the trip, he was ready to return home, for he was very thirsty, and his stomach was growling audibly. Some of his companions were taking regular sips of water or whatever out of fancy containers that looked like flasks, but none of them offered Austin a drink or even bothered to ask if he was thirsty. He took note of that and kept showing them around like a faithful servant. After every couple of steps, he would hear them shout "Wow!"; "Amazing!"; "Picturesque!"; "Awesome!"; and so on while taking pictures.

Two hours into the trip, the tourists decided it was time for a break. They chose an area with some gorgeous rocks to sit down and eat. They were all eating and drinking with relish and chatting loudly. Some of them even had beer, wine, whiskey, and fruit juice. Austin noticed that the two youngest members of the group, a male and a female, would kiss passionately from time to time.

His companions had been eating for about twenty-five minutes when he realized that they were not going to offer him anything. In fact, they all acted as if he were not even present and went on with their business. He sat there and thought about what to do. "Should I ask them for something to eat and drink, or should I just walk up to one of them and start sharing their food and drink? Maybe I should just walk away and return home. I have plenty to eat and drink waiting for me up there." After considering all the options he had thought about, he finally settled on a terribly mischievous one.

When the Europeans and Americans were done eating and resting, one of them had the guts to ask, "Hey, Austin, what can we see next?" Austin knew then that the time had come to teach those insensitive and ungrateful people a lesson they would never forget. On the opposite side from where they were sitting, there were the most beautiful flowers and rock formations in the valley, but the locals always stayed away from the area because it was infested with some very dangerous, gargantuan ants. Just one bite by those bad boys would warrant a trip to the hospital because the body would swell and burn immensely. The bite would also cause excruciating pain that would last for days.

Austin guided the tourists into the most dangerous part of the valley. As they were walking, he trailed behind, slowly, and just gave directions.

As expected, the visitors were so excited that none of them paid attention to the ants that were on their way. After making sure that the visitors were right in the middle of the ant-infested area, Austin climbed and sat on one of the rocks, out of harm's way. He could see the ants crawling on some of the victims, but he only tightened his lips to stifle the laughter that was about to burst out. It wasn't long before several of the tourists started twisting, twerking, jumping, and even rolling on the ground like individuals in a voodoo ceremony. None of them escaped the viciousness of the ants. Austin heard them scream, in pain, "Ants! Ants! Help! Help! Please help!" Some of them took their clothes off and started shaking them. In the midst of the confusion and trauma, Austin disappeared. He returned home, took a shower, ate his lunch, and took a nap. When he woke up, the buses were gone.

The episode with the tourists reminded him of a similar encounter three months earlier between him and his family's backyard neighbor, Mr. Mike, an American Peace Corps teacher. One evening, the neighbor was passing by Austin's house on his motorcycle when suddenly there was a very loud vrrrrrrrm followed by an even louder bang. Austin knew exactly what had happened, and he immediately went to get his father. "Mr. Mike has had an accident. He needs help," he shouted. Both of them ran as fast as they could to their neighbor's rescue. When they got to him, they found him lying on the ground, face up, with his very heavy Yamaha sports motorcycle right across his chest. The engine was still running, and the exhaust pipe had already burned his T-shirt in the chest area, and there was a brown burn mark from one side of the victim's chest to the other. He was letting out repeated "Ah bhuh! Ah bhuh! Ah bhuh!" as he was trying desperately to push the massive load of Japanese engineering off his chest, but he was no match for the humongous machine.

The Good Samaritans got to him before he could pass out. After multiple attempts, the father-and-son duo was able to lift the motorcycle and release its prisoner. They helped him to his feet and walked him home, the father supporting him on one side and the son on the other. After ensuring that the expatriate was comfortable and safe, they returned to the accident spot and pushed the motorcycle to his house. The teacher thanked them for rescuing him, and they returned home.

The next day, Mr. Mike called Austin to help him clean his yard. Armed with a machete, Austin happily did most of the work, since the neighbor was still in pain from the accident. However, when the work was almost done, the homeowner disappeared. Austin finished cutting the grass, raked everything, and waited for Mr. Mike to return. He didn't. So the helper went to check on him. He found the man sitting in his dining room, savoring his rice-and-peanut-soup dinner with obvious relish and gusto. He saw the kid who had cleaned his entire half-acre yard but did not invite him to dinner. Instead he gave the child a telescope to go look at the sky while he finished eating. Austin marveled at the closeness of distant objects for a few minutes and returned the telescope to its owner, for his hunger had become unbearable. Seeing his neighbor eating one of his favorite dishes only aggravated his desire for food.

The two encounters with the foreigners filled Austin with a lot of disappointment and disgust. He concluded that "white people are very stingy and cunning. They are scrooges!" However, he vowed not to let the incidents cloud his judgment about right and wrong. "The Bible says you should love your neighbor as yourself, and Papa always says that it is important to help those in need of help. That's what I'll keep on doing," he told himself.

He got home from helping his neighbor, took a shower, ate a plate of fufu and njama njama, and decided to hit his books for the second time that day. The new school year was just a week away, and, as far as he knew, the stakes were exceedingly high. He had to graduate early, at all costs. When he finished studying, he made some adjustments to his daily schedule, since school was about to start. The summer schedule stayed in effect on weekends, but on weekdays he was going to do the following:

5:00 a.m.–6:45 a.m.: Wake up, brush teeth, do chores (clean my room and living room), take a bath, get dressed, eat breakfast, and leave for school

7:30 a.m.–3:00 p.m.: School
5:00 p.m.–8:00 p.m.: Study (break for dinner when ready)
8:30 p.m.: Bedtime

Austin started sixth grade on September 9. He was very happy to be back in school to see his friends but especially to take a shot at going to secondary school early. His new teacher, Mr. Njeme, was about five ten and weighed around 215 pounds. He was always freshly shaved and had a penchant for fine threads. It was evident that he cared a lot about his physical appearance, and Austin wondered if his outward sharpness was matched by intellectual fortitude.

It didn't take long for his teacher to prove to his students that he was more than an above-average teacher. He didn't just have high expectations for his students; he also didn't spare any efforts and means to help them meet the expectations. However, Mr. Njeme was extremely allergic to student misbehavior. He would pull out his whip and administer a severe beating to any student who disrupted his class. That guaranteed a mostly quiet learning environment the entire school year, and Austin liked it a lot.

Through Mr. Njeme's expert instruction and Austin's discipline, hard work, and determination, Austin finished the first term at the top of his class. When classes resumed for the second term in January, he worked even harder, as, in addition to his sixth-grade courses, he was also taking seventh-grade English and arithmetic to prepare for the Common Entrance, his ticket to secondary school, which was just a couple of months away. The seventh-grade teachers offered morning and afternoon classes to prepare students for the exam, and Austin attended every day, even though it meant getting to school thirty minutes earlier and leaving an hour and a half later daily.

By the close of February, his dedication to school and studying started taking a toll on his health. He was having severe headaches that prevented him from sitting upright to study, but he didn't give up. He would study in his bed lying down with his head raised by a couple of pillows.

He was given a prescription for the headaches, and his parents tried to get him to study less and rest more. They even kept him at home on days when he got very sick, but on those days, the fear of falling behind and not being sufficiently prepared for the big exam made his condition precarious. He got so sick that he had to spend a whole week hospitalized. Unfortunately for the poor dreamer, that was the week before the long-awaited Common Entrance exam.

Thus, it was a partially recovered and frail but extremely determined kid whom the parents walked to Government High School, Mbengwi, the morning of the exam. The Common Entrance Examination was taken at the high school because it was the only location with enough space to accommodate all the students taking it. Even though he had not studied as much as he wanted in the days leading to the exam, Austin was still determined not to let his preparation during the weeks prior go to waste. He also had faith that God had seen his efforts and that he would crown them with success. Consequently, before his parents returned home, he joined them in praying for God's guidance and assistance.

The first subject of the exam was arithmetic. It had two sections: the mental and the problem-solving parts. Austin finished the former in time but struggled with the latter. He had a whole problem untouched when time was called. He hoped to do very well in English to make up for the challenges he had faced in arithmetic, but things did not go as he expected. He sailed through the dictation and grammar parts easily, but, because he put too much time into the planning of his essay, he was not able to finish that important section, which was graded for both completion and effectiveness.

As a result, he was devastated and inconsolable on his way home after the final subject. He didn't want to talk to anybody. When he explained to his parents how things had gone, his father, in his classic fashion, said, "Don't worry about it. That's nothing. You did the best you could, and God knows that. If it is his will, you will pass on either list A or list B. But if you don't pass, it will be the Lord saying it is not yet your time to go to secondary school. God's time is the best! Always remember that, son."

Those words calmed the kid down a little bit. That night, before going to bed, he prayed to God that if he could not pass in list A, which would guarantee him a free ride through secondary school, he would be grateful for a list B, even though it would mean his parents would have to pay for his secondary education.

The weeks waiting for the results were filled with anxiety, but he also understood that he could not let the Common Entrance misfortunes ruin his chances of going to the seventh grade. Hence, he continued to work hard, even when the results came back with bad news for him. With the unbending support of his family and friends, he took the failure as a minor bump on his road to better things and better times. He finished class six with a bang and promised his parents that he would sweep his way through the seventh grade like a tornado.

Chapter Five

Not What You Know, but What You Have or Who Your Parents Are

Class seven could not raise strong-enough barriers to block or slow down the tornado that came sweeping through it the following school year. Austin passed both the Common Entrance Examination and the First School Leaving Certificate Examination with honors. He could go to any secondary school he wanted. That year, he had developed a strong interest in a prestigious private school located about sixty miles from his parents. The Catholic Church–owned Sacred Heart College cost several hundred thousand francs CFA per year, money that his parents could not afford, even with their combined income. But they were determined to work harder, take out loans, and do whatever was necessary to realize their son's dreams. All he had to do was surmount the last hurdle, the interview process, to get to Sacred Heart. But the process gave him his first close contact with a cancer that was rapidly ravaging the fabric of the society and economy in Cameroon: corruption.

Since his parents did not have a car, they arranged for Austin to travel to the interview with a family friend who was an alumnus of Sacred Heart College. He was accompanying his son and two other boys to the interview. When they got to the school, Austin noticed that almost all the candidates were accompanied by their parents, uncles, aunts, and other family members. There were more adults there than candidates. They were all dressed in suits and other traditional Cameroonian regalia. He had never seen so many fancy cars in his life. The campus was heavily crowded and looked like a giant market or a trade fair that morning.

It was in a very clean and well-furnished classroom that the written part of the interview took place. Austin finished very early, with about thirty minutes left, and spent that time admiring the gleaming, freshly polished floors; huge, shiny, and spotless windowpanes; the bright lights emanating from the two rows of fluorescent tubes on the white ceilings; and the cream-white walls, which looked as if they had just been painted that morning. All those things solidified Austin's interest in the all-boys school.

Feeling very confident about his performance in the written interview, he left for the oral part with great excitement and anticipation. On his way to the room, he wondered why every candidate he passed in the hallway was accompanied by a parent or a guardian. Even the family friend who had driven him to Sacred Heart had his son's left hand tightly in his right hand, as if he didn't want to lose him.

There was someone with a list of names at the entrance to the room. He asked, "What's your name, young man?"

"Austin Martin Annenkeng."

"I'm sorry; your name is not on the list for the oral interview," the gatekeeper said, and he dismissed the shocked, confused, and distraught teenager with a shove. He didn't give Austin the time to ask why his name was not on the list or what criteria were used to select the candidates whose names were on the list.

When the oral interview started, all the rejected candidates were moved to a separate room, where the severely alarmed Austin decided to find out what had just happened. He quickly discovered that all of them in the room had three main characteristics in common: their dads were not Sacred Heart alumni, they did not have other family members or friends who were ex-students of the elite school, and they were all economically disadvantaged.

Austin had just learned his first lesson about the importance of a richly fruitful family tree and/or an inundated bank account in Cameroon.

They were more valuable, more powerful, and more influential than even the brains of Descartes and Pascal combined.

When he got home, he unloaded a volley of why questions on his parents, and they did their best to answer them to console their troubled and disappointed son. For instance, he wondered why candidates who had passed the Common Entrance Examination on list A and whose parents were willing to make excruciating sacrifices to pay the tuition at Sacred Heart were overlooked in favor of lower-performing students on list B.

"That's nothing. Look at it as God's will, son. Everything will be just fine," his father said. He encouraged him to go to his second choice, Government High School, Mbengwi. It had two advantages: it was free, and he would stay at home with his very supportive family.

All three of the other candidates who had gone with Austin to the Sacred Heart interview were successful, even though none of them had passed the Common Entrance on list A. Their parents were former students of the school, and all of them had important positions in society.

Chapter Six

Summer with Grannies

The summer before Austin started secondary school was particularly exciting and thrilling. In July, he was allowed to visit his maternal and paternal grandparents in Dchang, his parents' hometown, for the first time. He had never been there, and, owing to his outstanding graduation from primary school, his parents decided to reward him with the trip.

After traveling alone for three and a half hours, he made it to Dchang one Saturday at around 2:15 p.m., and his maternal grandmother was waiting impatiently for him at the bus station. The birthplace of his parents was significantly larger than Mbengwi, better developed, and more prosperous. The roads were tarred, the buildings were well designed, the people were well dressed, and the streets were crowded all the time.

On their way home from the bus stop, Austin and his grandmother passed by a large lake where kids his age were swimming joyfully, individuals were fishing effortlessly, amateurs were canoeing excitedly, and lovers were relaxing romantically on the banks. The surroundings of the lake looked carefully manicured. There were also a dozen individuals doing laundry on the banks of the lake. It looked like a multipurpose location where the locals spent many hours daily.

When they got to his grandmother's Tsinbing village, Austin noticed that a vast majority of the homes had graves in front of them, and that scared him immensely. All the houses also had a family garden or farm with crops such as corn, beans, groundnuts, soybeans, pumpkins, plantains, bananas, coffee, and numerous kinds of green vegetables growing healthily. His grandmother's mud hut blended perfectly with the surrounding homes. It was a two-bedroom hut with dirt floors. The living room, with a fireplace at the center, also doubled as the kitchen. The bamboo ceiling had several columns of whole corn tied in bundles of ten to fourteen. There was a tiny window in each room, but it stayed shut all the time, leaving the main door to the house as the sole source of light during the day or a kerosene lamp at night. Whenever the fireplace was lit, the fumes from it were overwhelmingly suffocating to Austin but not to his grandmother and his cousins who lived with her. He wondered why. He was not used to that kind of life. Although his parents' unfinished five-bedroom mud house was not great, it did have a separate kitchen, electricity, large windows, cement floors, and plenty of space.

Austin spent two weeks helping his maternal grandmother harvest crops from her farm, clean the house and its surroundings, carry water, and cook. He would go for occasional evening strolls around the neighborhood but return home before dark because the graves in the yards of homes created an eerie atmosphere and feeling in the neighborhood, at least to him.

Luckily for him, he had brought copies of George Orwell's *Animal Farm* and A. Conan Doyle's *The Adventures of Sherlock Holmes* to read in his spare time. He spent the rest of July at Nzong with his paternal grandmother doing basically the same things. She lived alone and was very happy to have someone there. Her house was not different from the one where Austin had just spent two weeks, but he was gradually adapting to the living conditions. He was also getting used to the pampering and petting from his grannies. It was therefore with mixed feelings of sadness and joy that he left Dchang at the end of July to return home to his parents and siblings.

Chapter Seven

Making the Best of a Second Choice

Austin started secondary school the second week of September 1986. He had come to terms with the rejection from Sacred Heart and was looking forward to making the best of his second school choice, GHS Mbengwi. Two of his friends, Christian and Stanley, also got admitted to the same school, although they were placed in form one A, while he was in form one B.

He made three new friends on the first day of school, Levis, Charles, and Alfred. He had been assigned a seat in the same column as these three. All three of them were thirteen years old, but they were physically different from one another. Levis was the shortest of the group. He was overweight and dark skinned. His head seemed to rest on his shoulders, for it was difficult to identify his neck. He was the canteen of the group, as he always had something to snack on. Charles was very tall and skinny. He had short hair, which he kept groomed all the time. He had a long neck that made his classmates call him the giraffe. He also had thick eyebrows and large brown eyes. He liked to tell stories about himself and his dad's motorcycle. He had a way of laughing that would distract the most attentive person on the planet. Alfred was the loudest of the group. He found everything funny and found a way to make a joke out of everything, even the saddest events. He was so light skinned that he could have very easily been mistaken for a biracial kid by anybody who had not met both of his parents. He was also extremely talkative. Additionally, his voice had only one volume, very loud, and that got him in trouble with teachers almost on a daily basis. He very quickly gained the reputation as the class clown, although, just like his three buddies, his grades were always above average.

Austin walked to and from school every day with his friends. They also were inseparable during group assignments and breaks. Whenever a teacher attempted to split them up, they always came up with questions that would leave him or her on the defensive, trying desperately to justify his or her decision, and in the end either the teacher would give up or the boys would simply get back together the next day. Their favorite argument against separation all the time was that they complemented one another and their grades would plunge if their group were split.

The first term was very good for Austin and his friends. They made mostly As in their tests and exams, but they started the second term with a great deal of complacency, which was fostered by the attention that they were starting to get from their classmates, especially the female ones. As loud as Alfred was, he would not have even known what to say if one of the girls had made a pass at him, but he was very quick to egg on Austin and the other friends to take their chances with the belles in the classroom.

There was one beauty who had caught Austin's attention since the first day of school. Her name was Delphine, and she had a twin sister in form one A. She was brown skinned, of average height and body size, and generously bosomed. She cut her hair very low on the sides but kept the top tall. It looked as if she ironed her navy-blue skirt and sky-blue shirt, the school uniform, every morning before school. She also kept her shoes spotless and shiny, and Austin had seen her several times cleaning them with a white fabric and checking her face and hair in a small round mirror during changes of class.

One Friday after school, Austin was encouraged by his friends to speak to Delphine. He handed his backpack to Levis, used his right palm to pat the sides and the top of his hair, checked his shirt and slacks, and dusted off his shoes. He wished he had cologne to wear, but Alfred assured him that he looked perfect and told him to hurry. Austin met her in the school yard right on time before she could join her sister and friends on the walk home. That would have complicated things, for Austin was very shy and had never spoken face-to-face with a girl he liked before.

"Hello, Delphine! How are you today?" he asked.

"Fine!" she said dryly.

"You look uniquely pretty and incredibly attractive. I would like to get to know you," he said. "It would be great if we could hang out sometime."

She was blushing and trying to put on a tough face at the same time. "I'll see. I don't know. Give me some time to think," she said.

But Austin, whose courage seemed to have taken a dose of steroids, stepped his game up. "How about I take you out to dinner or a drink this weekend? Tomorrow?"

She hesitated for a minute and then softly said, "OK!"

"I'll pick you up tomorrow at five p.m. Where do you live?" he asked.

"I live at Buckingham Palace, not too far from here," she said.

Austin knew Buckingham Palace very well. It was a student hostel housing about thirty students of varying grade levels.

"I'll see you tomorrow at five p.m. sharp. Have a wonderful evening!" he said.

"Thanks! See you tomorrow," she said before speeding off to her waiting sister and friends.

When she left, Austin clenched his right fist as if he were about to punch someone, raised it up partially, and brought it back down in a rapid movement, like a soccer player who has scored the winning goal at the ninetieth minute of a high-stakes match. He then placed his hand on his mouth and screamed, "Yes!" so many times that he could not even remember. His excitement was palpable. He swaggered confidently across the yard to meet his friends.

They inundated him with all kinds of questions: "How did it go? What did she say? Did she fall? She gave you a head, didn't she? When will you speak to her again? Can she connect me with her friend Elisabeth?" And so on.

"Guys! Calm down! I can't answer you if you're all speaking at the same time. Everything went well. I'm taking her to Blue Moon tomorrow at five p.m.," he said proudly.

Alfred didn't believe him. He was the Thomas of the group. He would not believe anything Austin said until he saw him and Delphine kissing or some tangible evidence that the encounter was as fruitful as Austin was describing. Richard and Levis praised Austin's courageousness and sought his help with their own quests.

Austin acted like a man on a mission on Saturday morning. He woke up early and started doing his chores. He was humming and whistling "Love Me Tender" by Elvis Presley as he was cleaning his room and the living room. When he finished, he asked his parents if they had anything else for him to do, and his mother asked with suspicion, "Why are you asking for extra things to do so early in the morning on a Saturday? Are you all right?"

"Oh! Yes, Mami! I'm wonderful! I just have this powerful jolt of energy this morning. Do you want me to go and clean up the store and the bar before you open today?"

"That would be nice of you. Thank you! But wait until after breakfast before you go."

"No, I'm not hungry. You guys go ahead and eat without me."

He headed to his mother's business premises, and, with Superman's speed and dexterity, he had the whole place looking cleaner than ever. His mother was very happy and full of praise for him when she saw the work he had done, cleaning up her store and bar and neatly rearranging items on the counters and placing crates and boxes in the corner. She didn't hesitate to respond in the affirmative when Austin asked, in the middle of the praise he was being showered with, "Mami, can I go and do a very important assignment with Christian in the evening around four thirty?" He had to strike the iron while it was still hot. She might not have allowed him to go if he had come back hours later, or she might have asked him a string of questions and even given him some stiff conditions before letting him go. With his mother's approval, he went back home and informed his father about the homework meeting with Christian in the evening.

"That's OK!" his father said.

All he had left to do was take his time to prepare for his evening rendezvous.

He took a bath and returned to his room to get some rest. After two hours, at around 1:13 p.m., he read a few pages of *Strange Tales from the Arabian Nights* by Margery Green and then did a couple of assignments for his literature and math classes. By the time he was done, it was 4:00 p.m. He put on his best outfit and applied cologne right below each ear and on his shirt and slacks. With his immaculate white shirt, black pants, and black penny loafers, he looked as if he were going to church. He had to impress Delphine, who was a brilliant dresser herself. He grabbed his school bag to justify the declared purpose of his absence and left the house without anyone noticing.

He stopped at a fruit vendor and bought a few bananas and oranges for Delphine, as he had overheard her one day telling her best friend, Elisabeth, that she liked these fruits. At exactly 5:00 p.m., he was standing in front of her closed door, his heart pounding uncontrollably, and he tried to gather enough courage to knock. After about a minute, he gave his outfit a sweeping check and gently tapped on the door three times. There was a loud, squeaky sound, like from an old bed, followed by several seconds of rustling sounds, like someone rapidly putting on clothes. Austin could also hear several soft footsteps in the room, in the midst of which there were some murmurings. Then, after what seemed like forever, a male voice asked, "Who is it?"

Shocked and wondering if he had knocked on the wrong door, he checked the room number again and said, "This is Austin. Is Delphine around? I have a package for her."

The door opened, and a fellow whom Austin had seen a few times in form one A was standing in front of him without a shirt. He said Delphine was not in, but Austin saw the silhouette of someone who looked very much like her in the room. He was about to ask who the other person in the room was when the guy swiftly snatched the fruits and shut the door.

Austin stood there, dazed and confused for a moment. He couldn't believe what had just happened. He returned home, not with a swagger but more like someone who had gambled away all his possessions. When he got home, he went straight to his room and went to bed. He was not in the mood to talk to anyone. Later that evening at dinner, after he had not responded to calls to join his family at the table, all his mother could conclude was "Well, he finally crashed after all the cleaning up and studying today."

He acted maturely, surprisingly, when he saw Delphine in class on Monday. He greeted her, asked how she was doing, and wished her a wonderful week. When she tried to apologize for the missed appointment, he told her not to worry about it and that he understood. He didn't pursue her anymore. However, his friends, who had already heard about Austin's embarrassment over the weekend, gave him a hard time in class all day. Remus, the boy who was in the room with Delphine, had been running his mouth about the incident the weekend long. Richard and Levis laughed at Austin every second they could, while Alfred said he was right to not believe Austin in the first place. He also hypothesized that Austin had shown up uninvited to Delphine's place and, therefore, deserved what had happened to him. Austin didn't argue with him, for that would have simply prolonged the nightmare. By the close of that week, nobody was talking about the incident.

It was a very busy and eventful week, especially in his literature and math classes. In literature class, Mr. Kum's objective was to teach his students how to identify literary devices in a story and explain their effectiveness in developing the plot and characterization. In order to assess student comprehension of the devices, he asked them on Wednesday to write a short story in which they used any five literary devices, such as metaphor, personification, allusion, irony, paradox, simile, imagery, and so on. Austin's story was about a group of European tourists whom he had accompanied about a year prior to see Abbi Falls and its incredible wonders. The literary devices he used, seven of them, were very apt and brought his story to life. He got a perfect score plus ten extra points.

On the last class of the week, his teacher asked him to share his story with the class, and he happily went to the front of the class to do so. He captivated the attention of everybody with his commanding reading, but his friend Alfred was whispering something to Richard and giggling. After telling him unsuccessfully two times to be quiet and pay attention, Mr. Kum burst out angrily, "Alfred, I have changed your B to F." That paralyzed the disruptive student, and he could not even utter a word or raise a finger when the class rose in thunderous applause and praise at the end of Austin's story. The usually boisterous fellow was silent for the rest of that school day and on the way home. That made Austin very happy, as it meant that he would not hear about Delphine or about the incident in math class at the end of the school day.

That Friday afternoon, during seventh period, Austin got a whipping for not doing optional homework. He had completed the required part of the assignment but had left out the second part because the teacher, Mr. Fai, had said during Thursday's class that it was optional. However, when the teacher saw that Austin was among the few students who had not done the second section, he quickly changed his mind, saying, "Even though part two was optional, more than eighty percent of the class did it. That means everybody should have done section two. Therefore, those who did not do it deserve to be punished." With that, he took out his preferred whip, which he carried in his briefcase, and asked Austin and the others how they would like to take it—on the palm or on the buttocks. Austin took the five licks on his butt without protesting, even though he knew that the reason he was being beaten had nothing to do with the homework. Unless the meaning of "optional" had changed overnight, he knew that it meant he did not have to do the second part of the assignment.

Therefore, Mr. Fai was only punishing him for failing to run an errand for him the previous night. As Austin was going to help his mother close her business on Thursday around 7:30 p.m., he saw his math teacher loitering around the entrance to a compound where many students lived.

The teacher asked him if he knew Caroline, and he responded in the affirmative. "I need you to go and tell her that I am outside, and I want to see her," he ordered. It is commonly said in Cameroon that after God, there is the teacher. Thus, Austin knew that he had to run his teacher's errand before going to help his mother, but, because he was not naturally gutsy, and also because he was still reeling from what his friends had sarcastically termed "the Delphine fiasco," he went past Caroline's door and disappeared into the night. Mr. Fai probably waited in vain and eventually gave up, or maybe he went to get her himself, but Austin knew that the whipping he was getting was not unrelated to his math teacher's quest for Caroline.

The walk home after class was solemn. Levis and Richard shared a few words and picked on a group of girls they thought were not moving fast enough in front of them, but Austin and Alfred were mostly pensive. The former contemplated extensively reporting his teacher to his parents and telling his friends the real reason he had been beaten that afternoon, but finally, he decided to do neither because of the prolonged drama that might develop. The latter was very worried about the F he had been given in literature class and the impact it might have on his chances of promotion to form two. He eventually earned his promotion to the next grade, along with all his friends.

Chapter Eight

The Impact of a Bad Teacher

Austin liked all but one of the form-two courses. His favorite was English because he liked reading and writing. English also enabled him to express himself with ease and to understand the thoughts of others, especially those expressed in the books he loved to spend long hours reading. French was the easiest subject, and he made an A in every test effortlessly, because the French taught was too basic for him, and he spoke French at home daily since his parents were native French speakers. He hated math! Since the day he was unjustly punished in form one, he stopped paying attention in the math class, because his teacher had lost every ounce of credibility and Austin's respect. He barely passed math at the end of form one, and to make matters worse, he had the same math teacher in form two.

He did just enough in class to keep Mr. Fai off his case, and at the end of that school year, he passed math with a very dim D. Thus, Austin did not have a solid foundation in secondary-school math. It was therefore not surprising that he was mostly lost in form-three math class.

He had his most challenging moments when his new math teacher, Mr. Tambe, started teaching equations. After explaining and demonstrating how to solve equations with one unknown, the teacher asked if there were any questions or concerns. A hand went up at the fifth desk in the first column. "Yes, Austin," the teacher said.

"I am very confused. I just don't understand how you can add or multiply letters and get numbers. All this solve-for-x and solve-for-y stuff has my head spinning," Austin complained, visibly frustrated.

The teacher explained again with a couple of more examples and allowed the students to practice in groups with their peers, but Austin couldn't pretend that it helped. He tried extremely hard to bridge his math gap from forms one and two while following the form-three math standards, but, in the end, things just became too overwhelming for him. He failed math for the first time ever, but the outstanding grades he had in the other subject areas still kept him among the top students of his class.

That year he made a few new friends, including Divine, Eric, Valentine, and John. All four of them were hardworking students, but John, who was repeating form three, also enjoyed some wild extracurricular activities that were, until then, alien to Austin. He was two years older than his peers and walked with a slight limp. His hair was always cut short, as was required by the school. He kept his uniform very clean but never buttoned the last two buttons on his jacket unless instructed by a school official. Therefore, his bare chest was almost always exposed. Underneath his school pants, he usually wore at least two other pairs of pants and/or shorts—preferably jeans, for those were more valuable.

That was because John was an avid gambler. Whenever he lost all his money, he would wager his clothes or sell them in order to keep playing. He once lost everything, including his clothes, and had to borrow a pair of shorts to wear home. The gambling, which the gamblers called jambo, took place in another student's room at a hostel off campus. They would gamble in the morning before school, or skip school in the middle of the school day to go make some money, or right after school before going home. Most of the time, there would be five to ten boys playing cards and smoking and drinking alcohol for hours behind closed doors and windows. Occasionally, some tough girls were allowed to play, but the females who went to the jambo rooms usually went there just to accompany their boyfriends. Sometimes, amid all the drinking, smoking, and gambling, things would get steamy between the couples, and they would start making out in the corner of the room without anyone present finding it distracting.

John used to bring all kinds of pornographic magazines to class to show his new friends. He told them that he got them from the jambo house, and he often described with excitement and pride the things that went on behind closed doors down there. His detailed and colorful descriptions usually got his innocent new friends fired up and wishing to be a part of that tough crowd.

One day at lunch, Austin, Alfred, Levis, Richard, and John gathered under a tree behind the classroom to relax before the next class. John took out a magazine he was hiding in his back pocket and started showing and describing the pictures to his audience. Austin, who had never seen a pornographic magazine before, stared at the pictures and listened intently to John's stories about the happenings in the jambo house, such that his penis became as stiff as a rock. When his friends noticed it almost sticking out of his pants, they burst out laughing and making fun of him. It remained hard the rest of that day, as he could not get the images and the stories off his mind. It took a lot for him to turn down John's invitation to stop at the jambo room after school that afternoon.

Austin, Alfred, and Richard agreed to make a stop there—not to gamble but to watch and see some or all of the thrilling things that John had so vividly described earlier that day. As they were climbing the steps to the hostel where all the gambling took place, Austin suddenly said, "I'm not going in. I can't do it. My parents would kill me if they found out."

His friends tried to persuade him by telling him that nobody was going to tell on him, but he was not listening. He was already running down the steps. He was proud of himself for standing up to the temptation. Nevertheless, John's influence on him and the other boys would prove profound the rest of that school year and particularly in form four.

Chapter Nine

Dangerous Influence

When they all got to form four that fall, at John's suggestion, they sat together in the last seats in the back of the classroom, where they could talk and clown without getting caught all the time. That soon proved to be a huge mistake, as Eric, the extremely light-skinned boy with large gray eyes sitting right in front of them, was elected class prefect two weeks into the school year. Class prefects had several duties and privileges and a lot of power. They were responsible for taking attendance every class period and reporting attendance to the discipline master. They also watched for and reported disruptive students to school officials for appropriate disciplinary procedures.

It was therefore not surprising that Eric's first culprits were the incredibly noisy and disruptive boys sitting behind him. They just couldn't shut up for any reason on the planet. The first time he wrote them up was at the request of Mr. Bansa, the English teacher. They were talking as he was reading a text to the class. They were taken to the discipline office next door, where each of them received five licks.

After the brutal beating, John threatened to pull out Eric's catlike eyes after school, but that only infuriated the prefect. For a whole month, it seemed as if his duties had been narrowed down to watching only the five boys behind him. He wrote them up for ridiculous things such as coughing, laughing, sleeping, dragging their feet, singing, and being a few seconds late to class.

During their usual thirty-minute lunch break at midday one Tuesday, Alfred suggested that the boys make a quick rush to the monastery orchard to steal guavas. Although the orchard was thirty minutes away, they went anyway, knowing that they would be late to sixth period.

When they returned midway into the period, their problem was not the teacher. Eric had already written them up, but he had not yet submitted the referral. Nervously, Austin told him that if he did not report them, they would give him a few of the sweet and succulent guavas they had brought back from their expedition. A deal was struck in no time, and the boys were pleased to take note of their class prefect's Achilles' heel.

Every day for the next couple of weeks, they would skip fifth or sixth period or both to go to the monastery to illegally harvest guavas, strawberries, avocados, and sugarcane. Eric would get a cut from their loot each time to keep them out of trouble at school, but by mid-November, he became very greedy, asking for more than the agreed-upon cut. Instead of the one guava that he used to get from each of the five boys, he started asking for double the amount. They struggled to satisfy his greed on two occasions, but the next day, they didn't bring back much, because the monks who owned the orchard surprised them in the process of stealing the fruits. They were chased out of the immense plantation by the religious brothers with the help of their gargantuan and vicious German shepherds.

As expected, when they made it to school during seventh period, their class prefect had already written them up for skipping sixth period pending a "valid and reasonable excuse"—that is, two guavas from each of the class skippers. He was not interested in the excuse that John was trying really hard to explain.

"Ten guavas, or I report you for skipping class," he said.

Richard tried to show him the scars he had incurred from jumping off a guava tree and landing on a pile of cut tree branches, but Eric would not listen.

At that moment, Levis swiftly picked up the five guavas that they had given to Eric as payment for his silence, saying, "If you're going to report us for skipping, we might as well just eat our hard-earned guavas."

That made Eric very angry, and at the end of the class period, he went to the discipline master to report attendance and turn in referrals.

During assembly the next morning, Austin and his friends knew exactly what was going to happen after the morning prayer, the singing of the national anthem, and the reading of the daily announcements. The discipline master took the stage to read the previous day's discipline report, including infractions and consequences. The last entry on the report was the case of five form-four boys who had skipped their sixth-period class for a whole week. Even though that was true, the class prefect was supposed to report them for just one day: the previous day, since it was the only day the culprits were unable to provide a "valid and reasonable excuse" for.

All of them were suspended for five days with hard labor. Instead of going to class normally for five days, Austin, John, Richard, Levis, and Alfred had to use machetes to cut the grass behind the forms four and five buildings. They were also forced to dig the stumps of three freshly cut trees in the school yard, right in front to the school canteen, and remove the weeds growing in the midst of the yams in the school farm.

Surprisingly, the boys took their punishment without resisting or challenging the class prefect. All of them, especially Austin, knew that their grades would be fine after the five-day suspension. Austin's only concern was his parents finding out about the suspension. He was not lucky in that regard, because his French teacher informed his parents after noticing Austin's conspicuous absence in his class during the second day of the suspension. He was the most productive, the most participative, the most active, and the most assiduous student in the French class, and his absence could not go unnoticed for five minutes, not to mention an entire class period.

During morning assembly the next day, while Austin and his friends were loudly chatting about their suspension and what they needed to do to get notes and assignments for the classes they had already missed, someone gently tapped him on his shoulder from behind. When he turned around to see who it was, his face simply got in the perfect angle and distance for a dizzying slap from his mother.

"You thought I was not going to find out about the trouble you've been causing at school?" she asked furiously. He did not even have the time to respond or react, as she grabbed him by the wrist and pulled him toward the stage, in front of 1,040 students. The students parted like the Red Sea for the Israelites to make way for the furious mother dragging her son.

When they got to the stage, the discipline master, who already knew about his mother's mission to the school, announced, "Students! We have here this morning a very involved and exemplary mother who would do anything to see her son succeed. She found out that he had been skipping school, and she immediately rushed here to make sure that the skipping would not happen again. I need four strong young men to come up here to help this mother teach Austin a lesson."

At the mention of four boys, Austin knew what was going to happen, and he immediately regretted that he had not worn a pair of shorts underneath his school pants that morning. Before he could think about what to do next, he was suspended in midair, with a boy holding each of his arms and two others firmly gripping his legs. His mother and the assistant principal took turns giving him sixty licks with an orange piece of plastic tube, the type used in electrical wiring.

Austin was lucky that he didn't have to go to class that day, as he would not have been able to sit down. He could not go anywhere on campus the rest of that week without students pointing at him and whispering to one another. Some schoolmates were not discrete, as they simply pointed and said, "There goes the boy who got stretched in front of the whole school." Or "I bet he's not going to be able to sit down for a whole week." In every case of students making fun of him, Austin remained calm and ignored his attackers.

However, on the last day of their group suspension, the form-three biology teacher brought her seventh-period class to the school farm for a demonstration. Austin was upset because all those people on the farm meant he and his friends might not be able to finish in time to get their release papers signed in order to return to class the next day. While his friends stopped working to let the visitors go about their lesson, Austin kept digging the weeds with a shovel and shoveling dirt to put around the yam plants. At one point, he picked up a pile of freshly uprooted weeds to dispose of them in a pit behind him, but as he swung the dirt without turning around, it landed in the face and bosom of the biology teacher, Ms. Shelby.

Her pale-white Wisconsin face turned red, and she screamed, "Go get me Mr. Ako!" Mr. Ako was the discipline master, and Austin knew that was very bad news. It was never determined whether he threw the weeds on the teacher deliberately or not, but he had five extra days of hard labor added to his suspension.

His friends were allowed to return to class the next morning, while he spent one more week cleaning bathrooms, sweeping classrooms, picking up trash in the school yard, and digging up more weeds on the school farm. His friends helped him when no school official was watching, especially before and after school. They also had his back as far as notes, worksheets, homework, and other assignments were concerned.

They celebrated his return to class after his suspension with a huge and loud lunch at the school canteen. On the last day of his punishment, Austin spent some time thinking about how he was going to tell his friends that they needed to tone down the noise and disruptions, at least till the end of the first term, in order to catch up with schoolwork and improve their grades. He didn't have to tell them anything, because he found out on his return that the boys were well behaved and highly engaged during the lessons. In spite of the challenges, Austin was first in his class in all three terms, and he was promoted with honorable mention to form five, the last class of secondary school.

Chapter Ten

At the Threshold of High School

The summer break before form five was very busy for Austin. He spent most of his time studying. If he wanted to pass the General Certificate of Education, Ordinary Level, he understood that he did not have to wait for the school year to begin in September before starting to prepare. He had to start studying for that very important exam early. If he was not busy cramming material from his textbooks and notebooks, he was helping his mother at her business premises or harvesting corn, beans, and peanuts from the farms that his parents had. During the few leisure hours that he allowed himself, he went over to one of the neighbors' houses to watch television, since his parents could not afford to buy one for the family.

He hated going to people's houses to watch television, because the homeowners were hardly ever nice to strangers. "Perhaps one television in an entire neighborhood of more than a hundred households will make the owner of the television arrogant, disdainful, snobbish, and even mean," Austin thought. Sometimes, kids and parents from the neighborhood would fill up the television owner's living room to the point where some people would have to sit on the floor or bring their own chairs. On some occasions, the "rich" neighbor would not allow the "poor" neighbors into his house, and the latter would have to stand at the window to watch television. On such instances, especially during national and international soccer championship games, a fight would break out in the huge crowd gathering at the window, because someone was pushing or because some people could not be quiet while others were trying to make sense out of the faint volume of the television.

In spite of the bad treatment Austin and his neighbors suffered at the home of their more fortunate neighbor, they still concurred that he was not the worst television owner they had seen or heard about. There were mentions of a couple in another neighborhood nearby who would let the crowd of television viewers gather at their window and then pour hot water or grease on them to let them know that they were not welcome. The viciousness and cruelty of the homeowners grew exponentially if they owned both a television and a VCR.

Austin's father never left his house to go watch television at another person's house. He promised his children that as soon as he had saved enough money, he would by a television set for them. When Austin returned home one evening visibly devastated because their neighbor had turned the television off right when a musical show that the crowd had been waiting for had started, his father told him not to worry about it. He added, "If you pass the GCE, I'm going to buy that TV, even if I have to borrow the money from somebody." That encouraged Austin to work harder to pass his final secondary-school exam. When school started in September that year, he had read all the material for all the subjects he was going to take.

From then until the end of that school year, his schedule hardly veered away from studying. He got his friends to spend lunch breaks discussing schoolwork. After school, he would go straight home, eat lunch, rest for about two hours, and go to ENIET, a teachers' training college that opened its doors every evening, seven days a week, for students to study, regardless of the school they attended. That opportunity was an incredible blessing, as many of the students who went there to study did so because they did not have electricity at their homes. Fewer than 20 percent of the houses in Mbengwi had electricity at that time. Austin studied at ENIET every day from 6:00 p.m. to 10:00 p.m., including on weekends. Alfred, John, and Richard joined him there on some evenings, but one Saturday evening, he was approached by a girl he had seen several times before but had never spoken to. The girl, Yvonne, needed help with a pronoun-antecedent-agreement assignment. Austin was glad to stop studying to help her.

He noticed that she smelled really enchanting. Her chocolate skin was incredibly smooth. She had short curly hair, beautiful black eyes, dimples on her cheeks, and uniquely white teeth. The two top buttons on her shirt were unbuttoned and revealed her magnificent and voluptuous bosom. Austin struggled to keep his eyes off her breasts as he was explaining the assignment to her.

She was same height as he was, and her physique was made more mesmerizing by her impressive hips and long legs. Her high-heel shoes, short skirt, and detailed makeup betrayed her purpose that evening. She might have gone to the school to study, but she had also planned on meeting somebody. She told him that she knew his sister, Brigitte. They were in the same grade, form two. She also lived less than a mile from Austin's home, two buildings away from his mother's store. She had shopped there on multiple occasions, and she had even been to Austin's house to see his sister one evening when he was not there.

When they finished her homework, she said she was returning home. It was 7:20 p.m., and it was already dark outside. Austin offered to walk her out of the classroom as they continued talking. He reached for her right hand with his left hand and held it. She did not resist. He smiled. A few meters ahead of them, in the school yard, was a flagpole, the bottom of which had a round support made from cement and stone. The support was about two meters tall and the same dimension in diameter. The green, red, and yellow flag at the end of the very tall flagpole was fluttering gently and majestically in the evening breeze. Austin and Yvonne stopped at the symbol of Cameroon's independence.

She turned and faced him but didn't say anything. She just stared straight into his eyes. "You are mesmerizingly beautiful," he said inaudibly. She smiled as she moved closer to him. He put his arms around her waist and held her tightly while kissing her passionately. It was his first time ever holding and kissing a girl, and he did it as if he had done it a million times before. For about fifteen minutes, they just stood there, underneath the fluttering flag, she in his arms. He could feel her soft, succulent bosom on his chest while she felt something swelling progressively and sticking her between her legs, right below her stomach.

"How long do you have to study tonight?" she asked.

"I have about an hour and a half left."

"Are you sure you'll be able to concentrate?"

"You are remarkably gorgeous and irresistible, and it'll be hard for me to study after this, but I have to stay focused to pass this GCE."

She admired his discipline and determination. They kissed each other good-night and promised to meet again the next day after school. He would stop at her rented room before going home.

He managed to finish what he had set out to study that evening but not without difficulty. He could not believe what had happened earlier. He had held an outstandingly pretty girl in his arms, and he had kissed her. She had actually come to him and not the other way around, like in his previous attempts to get a girlfriend. "Unbelievable!" he said to himself as he packed up his books to head home at a few minutes to ten.

The next day at school, he saw Yvonne and three other girls in the yard in front of his classroom. They had come a long way from the form-two building, which was about three hundred meters away, behind the auditorium. It was obvious that she had come that far to catch a glimpse of her acquisition of the previous night and to prove to her friends that she was playing in the big league, dating someone who was three grades ahead of her. She saw what she was looking for right when Austin raised his right hand to wave at her. She ran toward him, leaving her friends behind. They hugged, shyly, as there were more than a hundred pairs of eyes in the yard at that time of the day. She told him she could not wait to see him in less than four hours. "Me neither," he said.

She returned to her giggling and praiseful friends, while his inquisitive friends, who were just an earshot away, did not wait until she was gone before they started grilling him with all types of questions. He told them that he had been seeing her for close to a month, and they didn't like the fact that he had kept Yvonne a secret. "What difference would it have made if I had told you about her?" he wondered.

When he got to her small room after school, she had prepared an omelet and a fruit salad for him. She set the food on a chair in front of him while they sat on the edge of her bed. While he ate, she could not keep her arms off him. She tried to feed him at least three times, but he wouldn't let her, perhaps out of shyness, or maybe because he liked doing things himself. Three more bites of the omelet sandwich, and he was done eating. They both then leaned back on the bed and stared quietly at the ceiling for about a minute.

Austin could not recall who initiated it, but they kissed and rolled in her bed, in each other's arms, for several minutes. Then she took off her sleeveless, see-through lace gown, and Austin almost passed out. "Oh my God! You're phenomenally hot!" he told her after recollecting himself.

"I am all yours if you promise to be only with me," she whispered in his ear.

Austin didn't need to hear that twice before promising to date only her. He had struggled unsuccessfully to get a girlfriend for almost eight years, and all he had gotten was ridicule, rejection, and dejection.

She was thrilled by his declaration and promise of profound feelings for her, and she pounced on him like a cheetah in heat. That was his first time having sexual intercourse but not hers. She claimed it was her second time, but Austin recalled hearing John say that girls always told their new boyfriend that their first time sleeping together was their second time.

"Every new girlfriend always claims that she has had sex only once before. It's the myth of the eternal second," he had said.

Austin did not care how many times she had done it before. He enjoyed it, and that was all that mattered to him. He continued stopping at her place every day after school for about a month until he was almost caught by his mother one afternoon.

He was lying in bed naked with his girlfriend after an hour of intense lovemaking when there was a roll of bangs accompanied by a familiar voice ordering Yvonne to open the door. He jumped out of the bed with the skill and speed of an Olympic gold medalist and swiftly grabbed his uniform, shoes, and book bag.

"That's my mother's voice. What is she doing over here?" he asked.

"I don't know," she said, as she rapidly slid into her gown while there was more banging and calling at the door.

Realizing that his mother was probably going to kick the door down if it wasn't opened, Austin slid under the bed, naked and with his belongings in hand. Yvonne then opened the door and pretended to have been taking a nap.

Austin's mother wanted to know if Yvonne had seen Brigitte and if it was true that the form-two students had had to stay after school the previous day to practice a skit for their French class. She confirmed the latter but said that she had not seen Brigitte since walking home with her that afternoon. Satisfied with the response she got, Austin's mother left, and he came out of hiding, beaming like someone who had dodged a bullet. He resisted his girlfriend's request for him to stay a little longer.

"I've to go study, babe," he said. "I'll see you tomorrow."

"Or, you could stop here tonight on your way home from ENIET," she said.

"I'll see what I can do."

He kissed her and went to his mother's business before going home. She was glad to see him, and after inquiring about his school day and about his sister Brigitte, she told him to take it easy with the studying, as he was getting very skinny from working too hard and not getting enough sleep. He smiled. "If only she knew what else was responsible for the weight loss," he thought.

Austin studied European history and did his biology homework when he went to ENIET that evening. By 9:00 p.m., he was done, and he headed home. He stopped briefly to see his girlfriend, who was looking forward to seeing him for the second time in twenty-four hours. She offered him dinner, rice and beans, but he told her to save it for lunch the next day. He was back home around 10:15 p.m.

With the same rigor, discipline, organization, assiduity, and resilience he had sustained consistently since the start of the school year, he made it to the last week in May 1992, the week of his first subject in the General Certificate of Education exam. The week started with his confirmation sacrament at the local Catholic church. He was very pleased to go through that significant Catholic rite, especially on the eve of the most important exam he had ever taken.

On the morning of the first paper, geography, he woke up early to prepare. The breakfast his mother made for him that Monday morning was particularly special, consisting of a few beignets, a thick omelet, a bowl of pap, and a cup of coffee. When he finished eating, he joined his parents in prayer. They hugged him and wished him good luck as he headed to school.

Geography was easy, and he was very excited about the possibility of an A in it. His next two subjects were English and math. The former was so simple that he made a bet with John that he would pass it with an A, but the latter was, as he had expected, a disaster. He didn't like math, because of all the issues he had had with his math teacher during his early secondary-school years. Not surprisingly, he expected to fail it. By the time he was done taking all the eight subjects he sat for in the GCE Ordinary Level, Austin could predict passing seven of them with a B or above. He would have to wait a whole month to know exactly how well he had done.

He didn't know what to do with the free time he suddenly had after completing the GCE. He had not anticipated having so much time on his hands. For a whole school year, his entire life had consisted of school. His girlfriend had gone to see her parents in Buea. His parents suggested that he could pay a visit to his grandmothers in Dchang, but he said he preferred staying put that summer. By the end of June, his maternally inherited anxiety and impatience were starting to manifest themselves tangibly. He started asking anybody he could find if he or she had heard anything about when the GCE results would be available. Even after many friends and family members told him that it would be sometime in early or mid-July 1992, he still wasn't satisfied.

Then on July 10, it was announced on the 3:00 p.m. radio newscast that the results would be published the next day and read on the national radio station. He didn't sleep that night. He thought about what he would do if he passed in all the seven subjects that he had not had trouble with. He also imagined a miraculous scenario in which he passed math with a D. "That would be unbelievable," he thought.

What made the night even longer was the nightmare he had when he attempted to go to sleep. He was standing in front of his mother's business premises on the first day of school, and his friends all had their new school uniforms and school supplies and were heading to school. They greeted him with a tremendous amount of pity and sympathy, and then Richard said, "Don't worry, Austin! Just study harder this year, and you'll pass the GCE. If you need any help, just ask. We're your friends, and we'll be there to assist you." He couldn't hold back his tears as his friends, with whom he had stuck for five years of secondary school, walked away to their first day of high school, leaving him behind to repeat form five.

"Noooooo," he screamed as he woke up with a start.

From then until dawn, he was wide eyed. He heard his father wake up at 5:00 a.m. to get ready for work. During the summer months, his mother didn't get up as early as his father because the beignet-making part of her business was extremely slow at that time. More than 90 percent of the beignet clientele were the hundreds of students and teachers going to and from the primary, secondary, and high schools. When these closed for the summer, that part of her business would shut down until the first part of September, when she would wake up daily at 5:00 a.m. to make the beignets for sale. On that June morning, Austin decided to help his father make his breakfast of tea, omelet, and bread.

"Why are you up so early?"

"I couldn't sleep."

"Are you anxious about your results?"

"No, I'm just ready for this to be over with. I want to know how I did. I'm also ready for that television you promised to buy if I passed."

"I know you're going to pass, because you worked so hard all year. I've been preparing to keep the promise I made to you."

Austin could not cheat nature for too long. When his father left for work, he got back in his bed and was fast asleep within ten minutes. His younger brothers, Paul and Kenneth, who shared the bedroom with him, were told by their mother to let him sleep. But at noon, Brigitte ran into his room and screamed, "Austin, GCE results are out. They're reading them on the radio!"

Austin jumped out of bed and ran with her into the living room and turned on the family's Silver AM and SW radio, which began spilling the results of center number 008. He turned the volume to the highest level. It would be several hours before the readers would get to his school, center number 044, but he pulled a chair up to the dining table and sat down, right in front of the door leading to his sisters' room.

He listened intently to the names of thousands of successful candidates whom he did not know while waiting impatiently for the readers to get to his school. His father returned home at 3:00 p.m., two hours earlier than usual. By that time, Austin was holding tightly to his seat to reduce the shaking of his hands and legs as the radio was loudly reading the results of center number 040. Austin would know his long-awaited results within less than two hours. His father sat in his favorite seat across from him, in front of the cupboard, where the radio always sat to his far right.

At exactly 4:21 p.m., they heard, "At this time we are going to read the results of center number 044, Government High School Mbengwi." Austin's trembling became uncontrollable as the readers went from the names of those who had passed in ten subjects to those who had passed in eight. He did not hear his name when the successful candidates in the latter category were called. That meant he had not passed math. The miracle had not happened. Then the journalist said, "Passed in seven papers: Austin Martin Annenkeng…"

Both his father and he jumped out of their seats screaming before the reader could even say his last name. His father hugged him, longer than ever, and when he finally released him, Austin saw the tears in his eyes. He had never seen his father cry in his entire life, but he understood that the tears were pumped by overwhelming joy. In one attempt, Austin had done what his older sister had barely achieved after three tries.

"Go tell your mother the good news," his father said.

Austin ran to tell his mother and siblings the news, but by the time he got to her business place, there was already a huge jubilating crowd of neighbors, customers, and friends there. They already knew. His mother and siblings proudly introduced him to the customers and other well-wishers who wanted to meet the star of the celebration. His father joined them later, and the business remained open until midnight as more friends and strangers came to congratulate Austin and to celebrate with his family.

The following day, Austin's father surprised his family at dinner with a brand-new thirty-inch Gold Star television set. Austin and his brothers and sisters were so ecstatic that their hunger simply evaporated. However, they had to wait until the next evening to see the first images on their own TV, because the set needed an antenna mounted outside the house on a ten-meter-long pole. The very first TV show the family watched in the comfort of their living room, on June 20, 1992, was *Teenage Mutant Ninja Turtles*. Numerous neighbors had gotten wind of their recent acquisition, and they excitedly joined them that evening to savor the colorful images and sharp sounds emanating from the black boxlike object on the cupboard, right behind Austin's father's favorite seat. For the rest of the summer holidays, Austin, his siblings, friends, and neighbors watched TV together daily, from 5:00 p.m., when the only channel in the entire country, government-owned and extremely censored Cameroon Radio and Television Corporation (CRTV), started broadcasting, until it stopped airing at midnight.

Chapter Eleven

High School

Austin started high school in the fall of 1992 with expectations, hope, and excitement. For the first time in his short academic journey, he could pick his own courses to specialize in. Naturally, he chose Lower Sixth Arts 1, or LA1, to study French, English literature, and European history. Those were his favorite subjects, and he had passed each of them in the GCE with an A. Those subjects were also a pathway to a future career in journalism, his dream job. However, his friends, John and Alfred, did not pass French and, therefore, could only go to LA3 to study European history, English literature, and economics. Thus, for the first time in five years, they found themselves separated academically, even though their classes were in the same building.

Another reason for Austin's excitement was the fact that the high school was on a campus on its own, completely detached from the secondary school. Coincidentally, the latter was at the bottom of the hill, while the former sat elegantly on top of the hill, between Chiguiri and the monastery. The high-school campus was just three years old. The buildings were ultramodern and included sophisticated science laboratories; highly stocked libraries with nice, comfortable chairs and tables; two tennis courts; a huge Olympic swimming pool; a large gymnasium with all kinds of sporting equipment; and fields for several outdoor sports, including some that were alien to that part of the world, such as rugby. There were also dormitories; a fully equipped clinic that had more equipment than the local hospital; and homes for the principal, the vice principal, and the discipline master. The main office was outstanding, and all the offices had telephones, even though those were extremely uncommon in the entire country.

Nevertheless, the main attraction of the high-school campus was the futuristic classrooms, which had what students called American desks, because they were the type commonly found in American classrooms. The desks had a basket under the seat for books. The classrooms also had closets and cabinets for storage. All of them also had a unique feature: a green board as opposed to the blackboards that were common in classrooms nationwide. Each classroom also had ten tall glass windows. It is an understatement to say that the high-school campus was the pride of the region. When its construction was completed, there were calls for the government to make it a university, because it was too architecturally advanced and majestic to be just a high school. To the secondary-school students in the region, the high-school campus of GHS Mbengwi was a major motivation for them to work hard, graduate, and go to high school on an ultramodern campus.

Austin's active class participation impressed and captivated his teachers and classmates the very first week. If he didn't volunteer to answer a question, the teachers called on him anyway during every class period to share his thoughts. It wasn't long before he made new friends in his class, including Eddie and Frank. He also noticed a cute and impressively attractive girl sitting three rows behind him because she would stare at him every class period, especially whenever he stood up to say something.

One Thursday, she invited him to eat lunch at the school canteen with her. He thought about the offer for a moment and then reluctantly went. He was hesitant because he wasn't sure if he was ever going to see Yvonne again. She had not returned to school in Mbengwi that fall, and the only means of communication with her was through letters that the extremely slow postal system took two to three months to deliver.

The name of the classmate who invited him was Sonia. She was the type of girl whom both guys and girls turned around to look at twice or more everywhere she went, because she was outstandingly pretty. After their first lunch together, she invited Austin to her home. She lived with her older brother and younger sister, but they were not home on the afternoon Austin went to visit. She sat with him on the couch while they watched TV. At some point, he reached for her hand, and she let him hold it. After caressing it gently for a few minutes, he moved closer to her and held her by the waist. She didn't resist. Within seconds they were kissing and hugging and caressing.

Thus started a relationship between the most beautiful girl at the high school and one of the geekiest boys at the school. They were inseparable on and off campus. With his help she was able to pull her grades up. She suggested studying together in the evenings at his home. That meant his parents would meet her and find out about their relationship. He didn't hesitate to introduce her to his parents. His mother didn't like the idea of some girl spending so much time with her son, but she eventually understood that her resistance would not stop them. His father, on the other hand, was glad to see Austin so happy. He was especially happy because of the fact that the two spending so much time together meant that Austin was almost always home after school, thereby making parental supervision easier.

Austin and Sonia passed to upper sixth, the final high-school-grade level, very easily. They both put a plan in place to prepare for the GCE Advanced Level, their ticket to the university. The stakes were extremely high, as, if they made it, they would be the first in their families to go to college. After spending eight hours at school, Austin and Sonia would return to their respective homes to rest for two hours before getting back together again to study for five hours.

On weekends, they studied two hours longer. It was therefore not surprising that when they took the practice or mock GCE in March 1994, they both passed in all three subjects with all As. That was an indication that they were on track to pass the real exam easily, if they kept working hard.

The two separated for the first time after they finished taking the GCE in June that year. She returned home to her parents in the Southwest

Province, and he would not see her again until fate would bring them together again four years later.

Austin's parents were incredibly proud of him when he left for the University of Yaoundé I in October 1994 to study bilingual letters. He was happy to leave extremely rural Mbengwi for Yaoundé, the country's capital, to attend the largest of the nation's five universities. However, the fact that he would have to go for months without seeing or talking to his parents and siblings dampened the excitement. He also found out right before leaving for university that his father had been battling diabetes and high blood pressure for at least four years without telling his children, probably because he didn't want them to be worried.

When he asked what those diseases were, all his mother could say was that they were the diseases that had killed one of their neighbors, a bookshop owner, a few years earlier. The picture couldn't have been painted clearer for Austin. He hugged his father that morning like never before, as if it were the last time he would see him, but the older Annenkeng told him not to worry about his illness and that he would be there when he returned home for Christmas.

Chapter Twelve

Country Boy in the City

Austin's initial plan was to rent a room at the student-residential quarter in Bonamoussadi, but when he arrived in Yaoundé, one of his cousins he had never met insisted that he should stay at her house free of charge. Even though her home was a long way from the campus of the University of Yaoundé I, Austin did not hesitate to take the offer, as it would help his struggling parents save money, especially as his dad needed medications daily. She also provided him food and pocket money from time to time.

To show his appreciation, Austin helped with house chores, such as mopping the floor, cleaning the yard, doing laundry, and helping his French-speaking cousins with their English assignments. Austin also liked the fact that his room was out of the main house, in the back. He was free to go and come as he wished. He could also do whatever he wanted.

He had class every day from 8:00 a.m. to 9:00 p.m., but there were long breaks between the classes. For instance, on some days, after his first class, he would have to wait from 10:00 a.m. to 3:00 p.m. for his next class. Since he lived almost an hour's walk from campus, he would hang out with some of his male classmates who also lived far from the university. They spent their time getting to know one another and debating politics, world affairs, religion, sports, mysticism, girls, corruption in Cameroon, and so on. They often talked about the girls in their classes and how to attract them.

Progressively, Austin developed a very tight bond with those guys, including Roger, Johnny, Luther, Jason, Victory, and Edwin. From hanging out during break, they started going to restaurants and bars to kill time. That was where he got introduced to alcohol. He had spent his whole life around it, but he had never tasted it.

After four hours of drinking one afternoon, Roger had a brilliant idea that would substantially increase the amount of money they could spend on beer and food. "How about instead of each of us buying all the textbooks for each of our classes, we just assign each person a course, and he buys the textbook? We would take turns reading the books, and that would be very easy to do, since we spend almost all day together anyway."

"Roger, you're a genius! You deserve a Nobel Prize for coming up with an idea like that," said Edwin.

"That means instead of buying seven books, I would just buy one, and the rest of the book money would be for booze," Victory said.

Austin, who was already adding the numbers in his head, said, "Well, if that's the case, I pick the pink textbook that the Simo guy is forcing us to buy. What's it called again? *Effective* something, something..." The six bottles of Satzenbrau that he had already downed were robbing him of his ability to think clearly, but his friends understood the book he was talking about. Each of them agreed on a course and the book to buy. The excitement around the table was electric. They decided to get one more round of beer for the walk back to campus, even though they had barely twenty minutes left.

When they got to class that afternoon, they learned that the professor had rescheduled the comparative studies class to earlier that day and had given a test because fewer than 30 percent of the students were present. In fact, only the class delegate and a few of his buddies knew about the schedule change, and it was because the former, who was same age as the professor and hailed from the same tribe, spent all the free time he had with the teacher.

A huge crowd of more than a hundred students had already gathered in front of the professor's office to contest the manner in which the class was rescheduled and to ask for a makeup test, but he refused to listen to their pleas. Instead, he informed them through his friend, the delegate, that he had the right to cancel and reschedule class at will, that there would be no makeup test, that they would get a zero for the missed test, and that they should clear the front of his office or else.

Austin later found out that the situation was typical of the University of Yaoundé I, as professors did not care if students passed their courses or not. They couldn't care less if everybody failed. They would still have their jobs, and they would still get promoted. It was also very common for these professors to force students to buy their publications, including many that were poorly written, hardly researched, and based on flimsy and questionable theories. It was not uncommon for students to fail the class even after spending their last dime on the teacher's scanty publication. The authorities of the university were not unaware of all the corrupt practices of their faculty and staff. They themselves indulged in endeavors that took advantage of students in every way possible.

What was particularly amusing and pathetic in the case of the comparative studies class was that Austin noticed that there were fewer people in the crowd each time they marched to the professor's office to ask for a pardon and a makeup. The pretty girls who had been in the group the first day were not to be found anymore. They didn't seem worried about the prospect of a zero, either.

That made Austin and his friends do some digging around. They learned that the delegate had negotiated some kind of shady transaction between the professor and some students. The details of the transaction were top secret, but one student who was angry that the original crowd had shrunk to fifteen or fewer mentioned one morning that he had overheard something about a room at a hotel.

In the end, neither Austin nor his buddies got a makeup test. They even asked in vain for an opportunity to make up only 50 percent of the test grade. That only bolstered their determination to pass the class, but it did not deter them from going to their favorite bar across the street from the university between classes. They would double-check each day before going, just to ensure that another professor had not arbitrarily rescheduled class at the last minute.

Chapter Thirteen

Home for Christmas before Exams

Austin had an opportunity to return home to his parents for Christmas on December 22, 1994. He had never been away from his parents that long. So, obviously, it was a very joyful reunion. His mother had prepared a special meal, ndole and ripe plantains, just for him. While he ate, he was asked questions about his studies, his living conditions, the food in Yaoundé, and his relatives. He too was particularly curious about his father's health. His dad responded that he was still struggling to get his blood pressure and blood sugar under control, but his daily medications were helping enormously, even though they were extremely costly.

The next day, the family spent the entire afternoon and evening preparing for Christmas. The guys slaughtered and cleaned three roosters, a goat, and a pig, while the ladies put up the Christmas decorations and got spices, condiments, and other items needed to prepare the entrées, main dishes, and desserts. The actual cooking would not begin until Christmas Eve and would continue the morning of December 25.

Every member of the Annenkeng family always looked forward to the Christmas holiday, not for the great presents they would get but for the fun and bonding the period brought. The togetherness was even tighter that year, as the children checked on their father more than usual and even attempted to take over his usual role in the Christmas preparations, but he insisted on being the butcher and the skinner in chief, saying, "I am still alive and strong. Stop acting like I am very sick and disabled."

The family fun and festivities continued with increased intensity for the rest of that Christmas break until it was time for Austin to return to Yaoundé to prepare for first-semester exams.

When the results of the exams were released at the end of the first semester, Austin and his buddies passed all their courses with excellent grades, including the one in which they had missed a test and gotten a zero. Their smart collaboration and gamble had paid huge dividends. It was challenging passing textbooks and notes from one person to another, sometimes in the middle of the night and when all of them were not in the same zip code. However, they resolved to repeat the same strategy over and over again because it was thrilling.

They liked having the extra money to party and spend on some new threads. By the beginning of the second semester, they were known in their class as *les six mauvaises têtes*, or "the six bad heads." They got the name because they would come to class drunk very often, but they would still manage to outperform the rest of the class in every assignment, quiz, test, and exam.

The second semester went much better than the first, because Austin understood the system better. He understood that the University of Yaoundé I did not have an established structure in any of the fundamental aspects of effective university education, including academics, human resources (recruiting, supervising, managing, disciplining, and paying employees), facilities management, school and community relations, admissions, registration, research, athletics, student services, residential living and dining, graduation, alumni services, and so on. Everything was chaotic and unpredictable. After just a few months of attending the school, students adapted to the rhythm of things and learned to not have high expectations from the faculty, staff, and administrators because all of them were too shady.

Austin passed every course in the second semester with ease. His friends did too. By then, their classmates had concluded that they were very smart guys who just liked to work hard and play harder. Their peers were right about the latter but got the former entirely wrong.

The truth was that Austin and his friends did not feel that their classes were challenging at all. In fact, they wondered how anyone could fail any of those superficial courses. The classes were incredibly boring, and the professors didn't care about their students.

It was 1994/1995, but most of them were still dishing out the same notes that they had given to classes that they had taught in 1978. Similarly, the textbooks that they used were from prior decades. Many of them shamelessly boasted to their students how difficult their classes were and how few students passed their courses per semester. Ironically, those mediocre professors could always count on the system to pay their salaries regularly, to promote them to higher ranks, and, in many cases, to appoint them to administrative positions in the university and in the government.

It was common practice for instructors to spend their time seeking promotions and appointments in the government instead of providing the high-quality instruction they were paid to do. Some even had unvetted and inexperienced substitutes and graduate assistants teach their classes while they were out pursuing promotion.

Since these mercenaries were always extremely scantily remunerated, and in some cases never paid, they were usually responsible for some of the most aggressive and hideous harassments of the students on and off campus. This went on with impunity. How could studies be intellectually stimulating in such an environment? One day, a patron at one of the bars Austin frequented with his friends asked where they attended college.

"We're at Yaoundé I," Austin said.

"That's great! You guys are at the mother of the universities," the man said.

His comment caused loud and unanimous alcohol-provoked laughter around Austin's table. Austin managed to utter, "If with all the corruption, abuse of power and authority, mediocrity, instructor insensitivity, harassment, and all other ills happening daily on that campus Yaoundé I is the mother of the universities, then I can't even begin to imagine what schooling at any of her five offspring could be like." The laughing around the table became even more thunderous.

Austin was among a handful of students who passed to the second year without having to retake any of the courses during the summer *rat-trapage*, or catch-up session. That meant he would have three months to spend back home in Mbengwi with his family. He used the time to help his mother on her farms and at her business premises. That time off was also an opportunity for him to reconnect with some of his primary, secondary, and high-school pals, including Stanley, Christian, Edwin, Evans, and Eric.

He also captured the attention of an extremely smart and pretty high-school student, Kara, who happened to be the daughter of his older sister's friend. However, after they had been dating for almost two months, the relationship slowly faded. Her family and his had gotten very close, thereby causing too much interference. The closeness of the two families also meant that they were seeing each other more often than he wanted. Additionally, she was a virgin, and that presented a different set of challenges that he did not have enough patience to deal with.

Of all the exciting and memorable things he did that summer, Austin was particularly proud of the time he spent with his father. They did simple house chores such as chopping firewood, cleaning the yard, storing the harvest, and renovating the house. Austin also ensured that his father's clothes and shoes stayed clean. In the evenings, his father would get him and his siblings to gather around the fireplace in the kitchen to roast fresh corn and cook peanuts. They would spend hours eating the corn and peanuts and telling stories and jokes. On some evenings, Austin's mother would join the fun after closing her business, but she preferred to let the kids enjoy their time with their ailing father.

Time seemed to be flying on an F-16 that summer, and, to Austin's chagrin, on October 10, 1995, he was back on an Amour Mezam Express bus bound for Yaoundé to begin his second year at the University of Yaoundé I. He had two days to get back into school mode and to hang out with uncles, aunts, and cousins he had not seen since he had left for Mbengwi. They wanted to know how his father was doing, and he assured them that he was doing better and was making great efforts to stabilize his blood pressure and blood sugar. They were also very excited and thankful for the gifts of fresh corn, beans, peanuts, and potatoes that Austin's mother had sent.

Chapter Fourteen

Bloody Academic Year

Classes started full swing on the first day. As expected, he had a more advanced level of some of the courses that he started during his first year, such as English literature, French literature, and comparative and contrastive studies, as well as brand-new subjects, including textual studies, francophonie, translation and interpreting, and commonwealth literature. All the professors showed up on time the first day and laid out their agendas, objectives, and requirements for the semester. The classes seemed to be more interesting and challenging than the previous year, although they still lacked the depth that he expected courses to have at the university level. Austin and his friends started spending more time in class and participating more actively in the lessons, but toward the close of November, things slowly took a very violent turn on campus.

The leaders of the student union started voicing the dissatisfaction of the students over some of the things that were making life on campus uncomfortable. For instance, there were no working restrooms anywhere on campus, except in the offices of the rector and his assistants. Students had to leave school and walk for several miles off campus if they needed to use the restroom. If the need was so urgent that they could not make it to the closest neighborhood in time, students would go into one of the nonfunctional restrooms to release their load. By mid-November, an immense amount of feces and urine had accumulated on the floors of the restrooms on campus, and the stench was constantly carried by the breeze into the classrooms.

The latter were also in absolute disrepair. The doors and windows of most were missing, while the floors were usually covered with trash, except when some dignitaries were visiting the school and the rector had to show them around the campus. Desks were missing in many of the classrooms, forcing students to sit on the bare floors to listen to boring and uninspiring lectures. It was very common for hundreds of students to attend classes in rooms that were built for far fewer learners.

The students were also unhappy about the unavailability of resources in the library, the poor quality of food served at the university restaurant, and the lack of space therein to accommodate the thousands of starving students. There were usually long lines outside the restaurant at any given time of day, and one could wait in line for three hours before making it through the final part of the labyrinth that led to the trays.

Similarly, there was the hassle surrounding school fees. The 50,000 francs CFA fee was extremely high for most students, as they came from impoverished backgrounds. Even when they managed to get enough money to pay an installment, they had to take a day off classes to make the payment, because the lines at the only bank the university authorized to receive payments were extremely long.

One Monday in early November, Austin had to get there three hours before the bank opened, and by the time he paid the first installment of his fee, he had spent more than ten hours exposed to the elements outside the bank. That nonsense had to end, the student representatives were demanding.

Other important issues that caused the rise in tension included student financial and sexual harassment by instructors and graduate assistants, nonpayment of graduate assistants (it was not uncommon for them to work for an entire school year without pay), and the low number of students passing each course. In fact, some professors often bragged about the insignificant number of students passing their classes, in some cases fewer than 2 percent. They claimed that it meant that they were doing their jobs effectively. How could a teacher be effective if 98 percent of his or her students failed? The students did not understand the logic there, but evidently the authorities did, as those teachers with a highly documented track record of mass-failure rates were often appointed to higher positions in the university administration and in the government.

When it became clear that the students' requests had fallen on deaf ears, they heeded their leaders' call to action. They went on a massive strike on the first Monday in December. They blocked all the roads leading to the campus; burned the cars of some school officials; shattered the windows and doors of the school buildings; and marched in thousands to the office of the rector, the minister of higher education, the prime minister, and the president of the country.

Those dignitaries promised to improve the quality of life on campus, but by the Christmas break, nothing had been done. Instead of the reforms promised, the campus was inundated by heavily armed soldiers, police officers, prison guards, and other civilians that the government desperately tried to use to quell the strike. It did not work.

The students started burning buildings and getting into violent confrontations with men and women in uniform. Hundreds of students were arrested, savagely beaten, and thrown in jail, but that only made the rebels more determined to achieve their goals. They took a break for end-of-year festivities and returned in January more energized, inspired, and resilient. The authorities decided to change strategy at that point, and they started paying some students to spy on their peers. There were also more plainclothes officers on campus and the surrounding areas, especially wherever the strikers gathered.

The brutality on both sides of the conflict reached savage levels by mid-January. One sunny afternoon, about a thousand fuming rioters gathered at their Carrefour Parlement headquarters to listen to their leaders, Schwarzkopf and Thatcher. News had circulated that the system was using student traitors and plainclothes law-enforcement officers to spy on the protesters. They were also angered by the intransigence and cynicism manifested by the administration of the university. The tension in the air was palpable as the protesters were chanting war songs while brandishing weapons such as machetes, knives, spears, bows and arrows, clubs, sticks, metal bars, and even some outlandish items such as car-engine blocks and dumbbells. It was very obvious that at that point, the protesters were ready to take things to the next level—to draw blood and plenty of it.

Schwarzkopf got on the podium in the middle of the immense crowd of thousands. He was flanked by his lieutenant, Thatcher, an interpreter, and two new faces. All of them were dressed in military fatigues. As expected, the crowd started screaming their leaders' names. Things were getting heated and electric. People could tell from hundreds of miles away that something ominous was brewing some-where in Yaoundé. In the midst of the screaming, the leader of the rioters started speaking.

"My fellow peers, we went to the authorities of our university to draw their attention to our grievances. We asked for common-sense reforms to improve student life on campus, to make the university environment more conducive to learning. They pretended to listen attentively to us and then promised to enact the reforms that we needed. They lied to us! In place of the reforms, they've been trying really hard to shut us up! Hundreds of our friends have been arrested. Hundreds more have been brutally beaten. Today I have confirmation that some of us have started betraying our cause and are working as spies for the authorities, alongside plainclothes law-enforcement officers."

The crowd suddenly became dead silent. Once could hear a pin drop.

After what seemed like eternity, the icy silence was broken by an an-gry voice somewhere in the crowd. "One of those spies is standing right here," the voice screamed. "He is a gendarme. I saw him with other gen-darmes on campus yesterday, and he had a uniform on, and he was car-rying a rifle," the voice said.

"Bring that mole to the front, to the podium," commanded Schwarzkopf.

There was a huge commotion where the suspected individual was found. His resistance was no match for the six heavily muscular guys who easily uprooted him and effortlessly carried him through the parting crowd to the podium.

The man was tall and very dark skinned. He was probably in his midthirties and had quite a few scars running up and down his cheeks. His very white teeth and eyes contrasted sharply with the charcoal blackness of his skin. All those physical attributes indicated that he was most likely from the northern part of the country and, consequently, French-speaking. Thus, Schwarzkopf asked him bluntly, *"Est-ce que vous êtes un gendarme?"* ("Are you a gendarme officer?")

The man said, "No."

He was asked a couple more identifying questions, after which the six guys who had transported him to the podium started searching him. The search revealed a loaded pistol, extra ammunition, a knife, a walkie-talkie, and a professional identity card issued by the Ministry of Defense. The evidence that he was what the voice had suspected was staggering. The man looked terrified.

"Get him out of my sight," ordered the visibly shaken leader in a stern voice, without even looking at the spy. At that point, the tension in the crowd had rebuilt and doubled. The gendarme officer was escorted off the podium and through the crowd. He was almost dismembered by hands extending from every direction, but his escorts managed to lead him away from the protesters toward the marshes behind the houses at Carrefour Parlement. It was unclear what they did to him there, but Austin heard from reliable sources that something was done to his head with one of the engine blocks that some of the rioters were carrying.

There must have been more spies in the crowd, because, before the leaders could dismiss the rioters to start exacting violence on and around the university campus, hundreds of heavily armed police officers, gendarme elements, and soldiers appeared from every direction. Schwarzkopf told the protesters to stay calm and that the intruders were outnumbered, but there is something about law-enforcement officials armed to the teeth with rifles, pistols, tear gas, water cannons, grenades, gas masks, and so on that makes even the toughest protesters think twice about resisting.

Chaos ensued as panicking protesters started running toward any opening they could find while the intruders were firing tear gas and rubber bullets at random in every direction. Within minutes, a thick cloud of smoke enveloped the protesters' headquarters and blinded everybody such that they could not identify who or what was in front of them. The widespread, profuse coughing of the protesters mixed with the gunfire; the bangs from the tear-gas launchers; and the splashing from the water cannons created a chaotic music for several minutes, at the end of which there were numerous protesters, including the leaders, arrested. Many others were severely injured, while one student was killed by a live bullet from one of the masked men. Thus ended the bloodiest day of the strike. It was called thereafter Black Tuesday.

Early Wednesday morning an announcement was made on the national radio station to invite all students of the University of Yaoundé I to an emergency-crisis meeting the following day at 10:00 a.m. to stem the immense tide. The announcement was jointly made by the minister of higher education and the rector of the university. It was repeated at the top of every hour for the next twenty-four hours.

Thousands of students filled amphitheater 1001, and thousands more gathered outside along the path leading to the building about an hour before the meeting. When the minister and the university authorities arrived, their motorcade was prevented from going all the way to the front of the amphitheater. That forced them to get out of their fancy air-conditioned limousines and walk for half a mile in the middle of the angry crowd to the building. As they walked, all kinds of insults were thrown at them. Some students even threw rotten tomatoes and rotten eggs at them. They put their heads down and silently endured all the insults and provocations. About thirty feet from the venue, just as the rector was using his enormous fingers to wipe off the thick, black rotten egg just above his left eye, someone shouted, "Look at his huge stomach! He could eat a whole pig and a turkey all by himself!" There was loud laughter and screams for several minutes as the dignitaries disappeared into the building.

The meeting was very brief. Both the rector and the minister promised to carry out reforms that would enhance teaching and learning and make life on campus more comfortable for everyone. They implored the students to return to class the next day. They announced that the first-semester exams would be postponed to make up for all the lost instructional time. The students demanded that all their peers who had been arrested since the beginning of the strike be released before they would go back to class, and the authorities said they would do their best to ensure that.

Classes resumed timidly the next day. Very little instruction and learning occurred on the first day back, as most students were just glad to be back, and they wanted to talk about the events of the strike. Austin and Roger described their adventure at a nightclub downtown the previous weekend.

The period of the strike was party time for Austin and his buddies, individually and collectively. The fun reached dangerous heights the Saturday before Black Tuesday. Austin went to the evening mass at the Catholic church at the Melen market. When the service ended at 7:00 p.m., he started barhopping just a few yards from there, at Mini Ferme. At 10:30 p.m., he took a taxi to a popular bar across the street from Cinema le Capitol. He had a few bottles of beer before taking another cab to Le Minaret, about two miles from there. It was almost 1:00 a.m. When he walked in, he went straight to the bar and ordered a bottle of Satzenbrau, or Satz, as it was more affectionately known, and a glass of water. He didn't pay any attention to the tall, slim, bald and shiny-headed fellow drinking alone to his right. Austin grabbed his Satz, and with one massive gulp, he drained half of the bottle. Then he drank all of the water.

As he went for his second gulp of the Satz, a voice coming from his right asked, "Austin, what are you doing out here this late?" No amount of booze could dim his memory enough to not recognize the familiar voice. It was one of his drinking buddies, Roger. He too was drinking solo that night, but fate had brought them together at the right time. They would need each other for what was going to happen that night.

They were kicked out of Le Minaret before it closed at 2:00 a.m., and they walked noisily down Avenue Kennedy until they found the only bar open, El Campero. The place was busy, with patrons overflowing the sitting area and using beer crates to sit dangerously close to the left lane of the street. That was where Austin and Roger squeezed two empty crates into a tiny spot in the crowd and sat down with their feet on the street. They would move their feet each time a car was approaching.

Somewhere around 4:00 a.m., they realized that they were both out of cash. They didn't even have the money to take a cab home, about twenty-five miles away. After contemplating what to do for several minutes, Austin suggested that they could take a cab and jump out of it as it approached Carrefour CRADAT. It was an extremely risky idea but one worth trying. They could get caught and taken to jail, or they could hurt themselves badly in the process, or both things could befall them. The risk did not dissuade them, especially as they were not in any shape to walk.

Roger stopped the very first cab that showed up and said, "Carrefour CRADAT, four hundred francs"—a little over the regular fare. The driver liked what he heard. Austin and Roger sat quietly in the back of the yellow Toyota Corolla, as if they didn't know each other. They were both praying that their plan would work. There is something about danger that brings a drunk back to his or her senses. The two friends were in a very dangerous situation.

At 4:45 a.m., the cab made it to Chateau and started easing down the remaining mile before Carrefour CRADAT. Before the car could come to a complete stop at the destination, Roger and Austin opened the rear passenger doors and bolted into Bonamoussadi, the student-residential quarter. The driver got out and attempted to follow them but gave up, perhaps after realizing that he could lose a lot more than the 400 francs. He could lose his cab. Additionally, the college students of Bonamoussadi were famous for protecting one another during the strike regardless of whether he or she was at fault or not. The two runaways made it safely to Roger's hostel, where Austin got some rest for the rest of the day before walking home.

When Austin and Roger finished narrating the events of that weekend, their other friends and a few classmates present didn't seem shocked by what they had heard. Their reaction clearly showed that they believed the actions matched the characters perfectly.

The semester gradually got back on track, and when it ended, Austin was once again very successful in all his courses. Without any changes in his lifestyle, he worked his way through the second semester until he was just one year away from becoming the first in his family to obtain a university degree.

Being in the final year made him start spending more time thinking about what he would do after obtaining his degree. He had had a strong admiration for journalism when he was in high school, but that interest had suffered greatly from his recent consideration of diplomacy and international relations. After graduation, he concluded, he would take the entrance exam for the International Relations Institute of Cameroon (IRIC), the only such diplomacy school in the whole of the Central African region. Getting into the school would be challenging, but Austin was not afraid of challenges as long as things were done in an atmosphere of fairness and objectivity. But first, he had one more year of studying to get his degree.

Chapter Fifteen

Graduation and Frustration

The workload in his third and final year was much higher than the two previous years. Consequently, Austin made the necessary adjustments in his lifestyle. He buckled down without relegating his social life too far down his list of priorities. The hard work paid off, and on the last day of school, he had the biggest party of his three years in undergrad.

His final exam was on a Saturday morning, and after that he joined his friends on a twenty-four-hour drinking spree. They painted the town red, going from bars to strip clubs and to nightclubs. They got so drunk that each of them got a packet of St. Moritz and smoked in the clubs. They thought it made them look cool. At one point in the night, Johnny was trying to stick a lit cigarette into the vagina of a stripper who seemed to be giving him a lap dance. The hard-core partying continued well beyond noon on Sunday, and then they all went and crashed at Roger's place in Bonamoussadi. Thus ended undergrad for Austin.

He returned home triumphantly to very joyful and proud parents and siblings. His father could not help telling everybody who would listen how his son had obtained his bachelor's degree without repeating any grade level or retaking any course. He told his parents about his desire to take the entrance into IRIC, and they thought it was a brilliant idea. They told him that they would provide him with the resources necessary to prepare for that and to compile the required paper work for the exam.

He spent a month in Mbengwi helping his mother at the store and on her farms and taking care of his ailing father. He also dedicated a couple of hours each day to study for the exam. One morning his mother explained to him the need for a plan B, because it was unwise to put all his eggs in one basket. He said if he did not get into IRIC, he would go to graduate school.

In mid-August Austin returned to Yaoundé to complete prepping for the IRIC entrance exam. He went to the school a few times to get additional resources and to talk to some students about their experience there as well as get tips to pass the exam. He was very pleased with most of what he heard except for the fact that there were extremely limited positions open for new students every year. An average of twenty candidates were admitted yearly out of more than ten thousand who typically sat for the entrance exam. Logically, that would make the IRIC entrance exam very competitive, but according to many sources at the school and around the nation, logic, rationality, fairness, and objectivity were not part of the vocabulary at IRIC. Although those findings troubled Austin, they did not deter him. He still believed that he could make it.

He took the written part of the exam on the morning of September 22, 1997. He answered all the questions very easily, because he had prepared for them. He met one of his classmates, Aurelie, in the hallway after the test. She spoke as if she were already a student at IRIC. Austin listened, astonished, trying to figure out why she seemed so certain that she was already in.

The oral part of the exam took place from 2:00 p.m. to 11:00 p.m. on the same day. Aurelie was conspicuously absent for it. Her name was called eleven times to face the panel of interviewers, and each time another candidate on the list was ushered into the room, as she was a no-show. When Austin's turn came, he fought back his nervousness and calmly answered all the questions posed by the seven-member panel. He left the room feeling very confident about his performance.

The results came out a couple of weeks later. They were read on the 8:00 p.m. newscast on national TV, and the twenty successful candidates were classified in order of merit. The first on the list, with the highest overall score, was Aurelie, the candidate who had skipped the oral part, which was worth 50 percent of the final grade. Austin listened attentively to all twenty names. His was not one of them. "Unbelievable!" he screamed.

He found out the next day from very reliable sources that Aurelie was the niece of the minister of external relations, where all the candidates from the diplomacy program went to work upon graduating. The sources also confirmed that there were also people on the list who did not even sit for either part of the exam. Their only qualification was their relationship to an extremely highly placed member of the government or their abyss-deep pockets. Austin did not have either of these, and the way things were, as he found out, he could take the exam a million more times and he would still not pass, even if he made a perfect score each of the million times. That was just the nature of entrance exams into professional schools in Cameroon.

IRIC and the other so-called elite professional schools in Cameroon did not have room for people like Austin, who were highly intelligent, goal-oriented, ambitious, innovative, and critically thinking young men and women. That discovery stunned and shook him to his core. He was so disappointed in his country that for several days he seriously considered leaving Cameroon and going to Britain or Germany or the United States. But he soon abandoned those thoughts when he realized that such a move would require a significant amount of money, which his parents certainly did not have.

Consequently, Austin resorted to plan B and enrolled in the master's program in English language and literature at the University of Yaoundé I. He felt very lonely, because his group from undergrad had disbanded, with all of them pursuing individual goals in different parts of the country. While he was still reeling from everything that was happening to him, his cousin informed him that he would have to find somewhere else to stay. That was a huge problem, since he had not factored the cost of renting into his budget, and he was certain that his parents did not expect that either. Finally, he persuaded one of his cousins to let him spend the nights in one of the rooms at his clinic. On nights when all the beds were occupied by patients, the couch in the main room was the most comfortable place for him to lay his spinning head.

He returned to Mbengwi for Christmas on December 23, 1997. He was very happy to be home. For the first time in almost five months, he ate well, got plenty of rest, and was able to have a clear head to recalibrate his thoughts. His mother advised him to consider taking the entrance exam into the Higher Teachers Training College, or Ecole Normale Supérieure (ENS) Yaoundé. He vehemently refused, but she didn't back down. She brought one of his high-school teachers, a close friend of the family, to talk to him.

The teacher told Austin, "Even though ENS is still one of the most corrupt schools in the nation, you still have a higher chance of getting in just with an outstanding performance in the entrance exam. That's because hundreds of candidates are admitted into the school every year, compared to IRIC, where only twenty are admitted annually."

Austin was still not convinced. If he had to list the careers he was interested in, teaching would not feature among the first hundred. He made that very clear.

Then his mother, with tears in her eyes, said, "Austin, if you will not do this for yourself or anybody else, do it at least for you father, who is very sick. Imagine what would happen to us if your father were not alive. We are already struggling severely just to afford his medication and have food on the table. Please, honey, think about it."

Even a stonehearted or heartless person could not be untouched by that. Holding back tears, Austin held his mother's hands and nodded his head in the affirmative.

Chapter Sixteen

The Unwanted Success

Austin left Mbengwi sadly on January 5, 1998, to struggle his way through the rest of his first year of graduate school. His classes were incredibly easy, but his living conditions were deplorable. He didn't want to tell his parents exactly how bad they were for fear they would worry themselves to death. So he kept on pushing ahead assiduously and resiliently.

In September 1998, he took the entrance exam to ENS. It was way too easy for him. He was not uncertain that he would make a perfect score or very close to it. After the exam, many people told him how foolish and naïve he was for assuming that he could get into the school without bribing. He even got an offer from an acquaintance of his older sister who claimed he knew someone in the higher-ups of the Ministry of Higher Education who could get him into the school for a few hundred thousand francs, far less than the million and above that other networks were charging.

"I would not have the money even if you brought the price down to five thousand francs," Austin told the man.

"You will regret it. This is a golden opportunity I am giving you just because I know your sister," the man said.

Austin thanked him for his "kindness" but reiterated that he could not afford the offer.

The results were released at the end of September, but Austin missed them when they were read on the radio on the night they came out. In class the next morning, three of his classmates congratulated him on his success in the ENS exam. He could not believe what he was hearing and dismissed it as some stupid joke. Then the head of the English department met him in the hallway and told him he was proud of him for passing the exam. It was starting to become credible. When another classmate from undergrad told him the same thing and added that he could go down to ENS and see the list with his own eyes, he took it seriously and immediately left school for the day to walk to ENS.

It was not a stupid joke. His name was the eleventh on the list. Although he was not excited about the school, he was proud of the accomplishment despite all the odds that were stacked against him in that exam. He said a silent prayer thanking God and looked for a phone booth to place a call to his father's office in Mbengwi. Some public offices in the rural town had installed phones to connect to the rest of the country the previous year. When Austin's father was called to his boss's office to take an urgent phone call from Yaoundé, he thought something terrible had happened to his son.

He said, "Hello!"

Austin immediately recognized his father's voice and announced, "Papa, guess what. I passed the ENS entrance exam."

Austin heard the receiver drop on the desk on the other end, but he could still hear his father screaming "Thank God! Thank you, Lord!" over and over for about a minute. And then his father returned to the phone to reaffirm his pride in his son and to tell him that he was leaving work right then to tell his mother the good news.

With the results thus released, Austin started classes at ENS the second week of October 1998. Prior to that, he found a part-time teaching job at Mevick Bilingual Grammar School, Yaoundé. Although he didn't have many hours to teach French per week, he made about 20,000 francs CFA monthly, enough to get his own place and still have some change left. The only problem was that he would have to serve three masters at the same time, including teaching, completing his master's program at Yaoundé I, and attending classes at ENS. He had completed the course work for the master's and had only the thesis left to do. At ENS, classes were not every day. That reduced the pressure on him, but he didn't hesitate to skip a class here and there just to make money to pay his rent.

He found a room at a very comfortable hostel below IRIC in Obili, Yaoundé. The monthly rest was 10,000 francs. He still had enough to cover water and electricity bills but not enough to pay for other expenses such as food, cabs to school, entertainment, and so on. He didn't care too much about these as long as he had a comfortable place to stay.

He hustled his way through the first year of the two-year program at ENS, and before the second year started in October 1999, he defended his master's thesis with honors. His exceptional performance spurred him to enroll in the doctoral program, fully conscious of all the challenges and scheduling conflicts it would involve. The year before had brought out the enormous gift of resilience and assiduity that had previously lain dormant in him. He was determined to take full advantage of them.

He was also selected as a graduate assistant lecturer in the bilingual-studies department, where he obtained his bachelor's degree, and in the bilingual-training units of the faculty of science and the faculty of arts. That was a lot of money, with the only disadvantage being that it was paid only at the end of the school year, almost a year after service. That meant he had to keep teaching at Mevick.

Running an incredibly tight schedule that left no room for fun, Austin completed the final year at ENS and his first year in the doctoral program. The final exams for those two coincidentally fell on the same day. Since the campuses were not too far from each other, he rushed through the exam at ENS, got a cab, and went to the University of Yaoundé to catch the last hour and a half of the other exam.

His results in the doctoral program were very good, but when those at ENS came out, he was missing a grade for a literature class. In fact, the entire class did not have a grade, because the professor, a politician and member of government, had taken the test papers on a trip to Paris and forgotten them in her hotel. When she returned, she bullied the head of department and the director of ENS into making the students retake the exam.

The problem was that most students had already returned to their respective places of origin. The few who were in town caved in and retook the exam. Austin was in Yaoundé, but he had other commitments. Even if he didn't have other things to do, he was not going to retake the exam without knowing his grade for the first time. It was not fair! And there was a law clearly stating that in situations like that, all the candidates ought to be given an academic grade.

The list of graduating students was published, and Austin's name was not on it, because he didn't retake that exam. That just fueled his rage and propelled him to seek justice. He complained to the director of the school, but obviously he was afraid of that professor, Dr. Akamba, because she could pull her political strings and get him out of his job. Next Austin sought and got a meeting with the minister of higher education, who promised to look into the matter but did nothing after forty-eight hours.

Austin decided then to turn up the heat. He passed through an acquaintance to file a complaint with the prime minister's office. On the same day, he went to the home of the secretary general at the presidency and waited at the entrance for his motorcade. When it arrived at lunchtime, security would not let him get close to the limousine, but, luckily, the boss of the home noticed that it was just an innocent young man trying to hand him something. He ordered the driver to stop and called on Austin to approach the car. He listened attentively to Austin's complaint and also took the written copy that he had in hand. The secretary general said that if Austin was telling the truth, he would take care of the situation, because it was very unfair. Not taking anything for granted, Austin then went to the most critical and most popular private radio station in Yaoundé and easily got an invitation to their hottest show, which was going to be live in the evening at five o'clock.

Austin did not have to go to the radio show. When he returned home at 3:30 p.m. to get some rest before show time, he heard an announcement on FM 94 requesting that he report to the office of the director of ENS as soon as possible. The announcement was repeated several times that afternoon, but Austin needed to hear it just once before getting into a cab and rushing to where he was needed.

When he got there, he was immediately led into the director's office by his chief of staff. That was strange. The last time Austin had sought to see the director, he was kept waiting for six hours. The director came from behind his desk and greeted Austin warmly and told him to sit down. Then he said, "Some of you think that because you have connections at the presidency and the prime ministry, you can come around here and tell people how to do their jobs. Well, your issue has been resolved. It did not have to go this far. All you should have done was come to me earlier, and I would have taken care of the problem. Your name has been added to the list of graduates of the fortieth batch, and your diploma has been printed."

Austin wanted to tell the man that he did not have any connections at the places he mentioned and that the director had met with him not long ago but had done nothing to remedy his problem, but he concluded it would be pointless. He was happy to put the bullshit behind him and move on. He thanked the director and left his office.

Chapter Seventeen

Chaotic Government

With the issue thus resolved, Austin turned his attention to his dissertation proposal. Graduating from ENS also meant that he would have more time to do part-time teaching pending his assignment from the government. All graduates from ENS were hired by the government and assigned to public high schools nationwide. There was also plenty of time to spend with the pretty Era, his new girlfriend. He loved and respected her even more for standing by him through all the difficult times. After his parents, she was his most valuable cheerleader.

By February 2001, almost a year after graduation, the government had not yet assigned any of the graduates of the fortieth batch. It was both good and bad news for Austin. It meant he had more time to be in Yaoundé to pursue his doctoral program, but the longer they were unassigned, the more money they were losing, as they would be paid only for time served. The always-calculating and innovative Austin found a way to make ends meet with less struggling than he had been enduring.

On February 14, 2001, he defended his dissertation proposal. On the same day, he had an offer to teach at a private university in Yaoundé called Institut Ndi Samba Supérieur. Since the hourly pay was much greater than at Mevick, he immediately resigned from the latter. He also continued teaching at the University of Yaoundé I, although the pay was still at the end of the school year. He thought it was incredibly ridiculous and stupid for a university to allow its instructors to teach without pay for an entire school year, because it promoted the temptation to engage in corrupt practices.

One day at lunch, Austin thought of a way to make some extra money to survive, especially as six months earlier, he had told his parents not to bother about providing him with any kind of assistance. He was going to fend for himself. He decided to put together a pamphlet, which he aptly named *The Bilingual Training Guide*. He sold it to his students at the University of Yaoundé I. The idea was a winner. It sold like candy during Halloween.

There were still no assignments for his graduating class by July 2001, but in early August, he found out that finishing touches were being made on the list. He was also told that if he wanted to be assigned to a public school in Yaoundé, which he desperately needed in order to finish his PhD and maintain his part-time positions at the two universities, he would have to cough up 500,000 francs. But there were two problems: there was no guarantee the senior government official asking for the money would actually secure him an assignment in Yaoundé, and he did not have that much money saved at the time. He was making enough money to take care of all his living expenses and set some aside for entertainment. So he told the man he was going to take his chances. The man asked him, in a veiled threat, "You do not want to end up in a faraway place like Kousséri or Akwaya, do you?" Austin brushed him off and left.

The following week, the assignments were published, and, coincidentally, the same classmate who had confirmed to Austin more than three years prior that he had passed the entrance into ENS stuck his head out of a passing cab and shouted, "Austin, have you heard that you've been posted to Government High School Kousséri?"

Austin immediately took a cab to the Ministry of National Education, where he saw his assignment. It was not a joke. He had indeed been posted to Kousséri, a desert town, the last Cameroonian locality on the border between Cameroon and Chad, a war-torn country. He suspected the government official who had asked him for bribe had had a hand in his assignment, which sounded like more of punishment than a job offer. He had two weeks to pack up and travel to Kousséri.

Austin met Era and his older sister for dinner later that day and broke the news to them. It was supposed to be a celebration, but they ate quietly until Era asked, "So what's your plan? I know you have a plan to deal with this mess."

"Well," he said, "since it'll be another year before the government pays me a dime, I will just go and assume service in Kousséri and tell the principal I can't stay one more day until I have a salary to sustain me. What do they expect me to eat up there, desert sand? Am I supposed to be drinking camel pee up there, or what? Where will I be staying? This doesn't make any sense!"

As thousands of past ENS graduates in his situation had done, Austin assumed duty and left, promising to return once his salary situation was fixed. It took him fifty-two hours on torturous roads and railways to travel the 1,376.5 kilometers to Kousséri and much longer, three days, to cover the same distance back to Yaoundé. He told Era and his parents, "It was like traveling to hell and back." He told them that the principal was very angry, but he could not make someone's child stay in such a hostile place without any money.

Austin returned to teaching in Yaoundé the next day and continued collecting data for his dissertation. Life was back to normal. Even a year after the postings, his salary was not yet out, but he knew that it would be a huge sum, because it was effective from the day of the posting.

One day in October 2002, while he was doing online research for his PhD thesis, he stumbled upon an exchange-teacher program with the Amity Institute in the United States. He read all the program criteria and realized that he met every single one of them. Consequently, he decided to give it a shot, but when he did not get a response after three months, he stopped thinking about the program. He concluded that it must have been a scam.

In mid-2003, the first group in his ENS graduating class got their salary. It was a huge lump sum. That gave Austin hope that his was coming soon, but it did not. He found out in July that year that his father would be retiring on December 31, 2003, and that his illness was getting more serious. His parents were already struggling to make ends meet. He was very frustrated that he didn't have the money to help them. He hoped and prayed that God would lead them through the tough times.

September came, and still no salary. Then October came and painfully faded away. The first week in November, Austin received a letter from Amity Institute informing him that he had been selected to join the exchange-teacher program. His assignment papers and visa documents were in the mail. His entire family and Era were very pleased by the news. His documents arrived by FedEx two days later. He had been invited to teach French in the Indianola School District in Indianola, Mississippi. He did not know where that was, but he didn't care, as he was certain that anywhere in the United States would be a million times better than everywhere in Cameroon.

Finally, on December 15, 2003, he received the sum of 3.5 million francs as his salary for the more than two years that he was supposed to be in Kousséri. He used some of it to purchase a flight ticket and a few items to travel to the United States and gave the rest of the money to his parents. He left Cameroon on December 26, 2003.

Chapter Eighteen

Culture Shock

Austin's Royal Dutch flight arrived at New York JFK Airport at 5:15 p.m. on December 27. He had caught that flight at Schiphol, Amsterdam, after departing from Douala the previous day with the same airline. He was impressed by the neatness of the airport in Amsterdam and especially in New York. The two airports also contrasted sharply with the Doula International Airport in terms of organization, service, comfort, control, and safety.

He almost missed his flight to Amsterdam because the police officers at the airport in Douala wanted him to provide a veterinary certificate. He told them he did not have one because he was not an animal nor was he traveling with any animals. They told him it did not matter. He needed to supply one or go get one from the nearest veterinary, at least fifteen miles away, return to the airport, and present it before he could board the plane, which was due to depart in less than an hour. However, there was another option: he could pay the police officers 30,000 francs, and they would issue him a veterinary certificate on the spot, and he could get on his flight on time. He was cornered. Realizing that he did not have a choice and that the cops did not give a shit if he missed his flight, he gave them what they wanted.

But at Schiphol and JFK, everything was smooth and fluid. He was in and out of both airports without any headache. Everybody was nice, courteous, helpful, and welcoming. Austin was impressed and excited about the prospect of life in a country where one could progress as far as one's capabilities could take him or her. The thought of that brought a wide smile to his face. Another surprise was waiting for him right outside JFK.

When he got his luggage and walked out of the airport to catch a taxi to LaGuardia, an awful-looking and exceptionally shabby man in his late forties approached him and said, "Hey, man, help a brother out with a quarter or something." He looked as if he had not shaved and had not taken a bath in a very long time. His pants, jacket, and shirt were threadbare. He did not have any shoes on. Vapor poured out of his mouth and nostrils with every word he said and every breath he took. He was not dressed for the weather on that December evening in New York City, and the bitter cold was taking a serious toll on him. He was in a very bad shape, but none of the people who passed by seemed to care about his condition. Many paused to stare at him before rushing into the cold, dark evening.

Austin had not expected to find homeless people in the United States, especially in New York. What shocked him the most was the reactions of the passersby. He thought that in "the land of milk and honey," there would be plenty for everybody, and people would be more sensitive to the plight of a fellow human, especially one in distress.

Austin did not know what a quarter was, but he suspected that the man wanted money. He had changed his CFA francs into dollars in Cameroon before leaving, so he reached into his pocket and pulled out the change he had been given moments earlier when he had paid for a packet of gum with a twenty-dollar bill. He gave all the sixteen dollars and some change to the man. "Thank you, man! Thank you, my brother! Thank you! Thank you!" the man kept repeating.

In the taxi to LaGuardia, where he had to catch a flight for Atlanta, Georgia, Austin wondered why the American TV shows and movies he had seen in Africa did not show that other part of America that he had just witnessed. Was that just a rare occurrence, or was he going to see more of it?

He arrived at Hartsfield-Jackson International Airport, Atlanta, at 11:55 p.m. and was picked up by Era's older brother. He spent the next twelve days touring the great city of Atlanta. It was slower paced and less cold than New York City, but unlike the latter, where he had noticed many people walking on the streets, there was hardly anyone walking on the streets in the former.

One afternoon, as Austin was walking home from the Bahama Breeze restaurant in Alpharetta, a car pulled over right by him, and the female driver asked, "Sir, do you need a ride? It's very cold out here, and I noticed that you don't have anything warm."

He thanked the lady for the offer and said, "I live in the apartment complex across the street." He thought it was very kind of the lady to offer a ride to a total stranger.

The following day, after applying for his Social Security card, he decided to spend the rest of the day sightseeing. He had heard that the world headquarters of the Coca-Cola Company were in midtown Atlanta. He thought it would be a great place to visit, so he took a taxi for 1 Coca-Cola PLZ NW.

There were many people touring the impressive piece of architecture on that day, as one would expect for such a renowned international company. He followed the crowd, which was led by a guide, a lady in her sixties, to several locations in the building that were open to the public. Then he left the group to take the elevator to the second floor. He got to the elevator right on time before the door could close, and he was glad that it was almost empty. There were only two white ladies, in their late twenties or early thirties, in the elevator about to take a ride upstairs. They had seemed to be in a hurry when they had passed Austin less than a minute earlier, but when he got on the elevator, they both looked at each other in disappointment and then got out before the door closed. "They must have forgotten something," he thought. He spent close to another hour at the Coca-Cola headquarters before taking another cab back to Alpharetta.

On Thursday, January 8, 2004, Austin boarded a Greyhound bus for a very long trip to Indianola, Mississippi. When the bus drove out of Atlanta, it began a sometimes-boring ride through cities and rural areas in Georgia, Alabama, and Mississippi. The names of some of the cities were familiar, such as Birmingham and Tuscaloosa, Alabama. He had read about them in books and had seen a couple of movies made there.

Mississippi State University in Starkville and Mississippi University for Women in Columbus were some of the attractions that caught his attention when the bus got to Mississippi. Then the coach drove into the Mississippi Delta, and Austin was amazed at the sights on both sides of the road. As far as the eye could see, there was just flat terrain covered with what looked like a cotton crop. "This side of America is extremely different from what I saw on TV and movies in Cameroon," he thought. "There are no skyscrapers, jets, limousines, sports cars, boats, busy streets, fancy boutiques, amusement parks, and thrilling-looking clubs around here like on the videos." For the first time since he had left Cameroon almost two weeks prior, he became concerned about where he was headed.

At 6:13 p.m., the bus finally made it to the bus stop on Highway 49 in Indianola. The French teacher at Gentry High School had brought a couple of her students to pick him up. "Welcome to Indianola, Mississippi, Mr. Annenkeng," Mrs. Tate said with tremendous excitement. "How was your trip?" she and her students asked in unison, as if they had rehearsed it.

"Long and exhausting, but I'm glad to be finally here," Austin said.

The students put his luggage in some kind of sedan, a Ford Taurus or something, and then the party of four got in the car. "We're going to the school. There's a huge crowd there waiting to meet you. The whole city will be out there tonight for an important basketball game, and the principal intends to introduce you at halftime," Mrs. T said.

Not sure exactly what to say, Austin responded, "OK!" before turning around and asking one of the students, whose pendant had caught his attention minutes earlier. "Is that a picture of you when you were a baby?"

"No, this is a picture of my daughter that goes with me everywhere. She's almost two years old," she said.

Austin was shocked by what the very short, light-skinned, curly-haired, baby-faced, childish teenager had just said. She did not seem to be more than sixteen years old, and that would mean that she had her almost-two-year-old child when she was thirteen or barely fourteen.

Mrs. Tate noticed the astonishment on Austin's face and understood what was going on in his head. "Teenage pregnancy is not common in Cameroon, is it?" she asked.

Austin told them that it was very rare, as culturally, individuals were required to get married before having children. Those who did not live up to expectations were highly frowned upon, considered to be immoral, and treated like outcasts for bringing shame and disgrace to the family name.

He told them about teenage girls being expelled from high school for getting pregnant. The schools were sending a very strong message condemning teenage pregnancy and premarital childbearing. They wanted to know if the boys were expelled as well, and he told them hardly. He also told them that in the rare cases of teenage pregnancy, the girl's family would file charges against the male and force him to marry her.

"Well, many of the students at Gentry High are parents. Some have more than one child. Therefore, you will find a lot of very young mothers and single parents in this area. I know several grandparents in Indianola who are barely thirty years old," Mrs. Tate said. Then she asked, "Are you married? Do you have any kids?"

"No, I don't have any kids yet because I am not married," Austin said.

The other passengers were surprised by his response, and the teenage mother asked, "How old are you, Mr. Annenkeng?"

"I'm twenty-seven," he replied.

The other passenger covered her mouth with her palm and then said, "You're two years older than my brother, but he already has fourteen children by eleven different women. He calls it spreading his seeds. You need to start spreading your seeds too, Mr. A."

Austin gasped. He was speechless. As the car pulled up in front of the gymnasium at Gentry, his mind was elsewhere. He was blown away by what the student had just said about her brother. He was mentally adding up the time it would take someone to have fourteen children by the age of twenty-five, and the arithmetic was not looking pretty. He also wondered how he was providing for those children, how on earth he could be a good father to them, and if the mothers of these children knew one another. That would be inevitable in a little town such as Indianola. Some of them might even be friends and members of the same family. The more he thought about the twenty-five-year-old father of fourteen, the more precarious it seemed.

Austin alighted from the car and swept around the fifty-two-year-old school campus with his eyes. He counted five buildings. There were hundreds of cars parked everywhere, and people were streaming into the gym in large numbers. The game pitting Gentry High against Greenville Weston High was about to begin.

The fans of both teams were seated on opposite sides of the court, with neatly dressed cheerleaders clad in colors representing their respective schools chanting and dancing on the sideline in front of them. Both teams were also warming up on the court. Austin had never seen that kind of ambience and support for high-school teams.

The game started at exactly 7:00 p.m. to the chanting, screaming, dancing, aahs, and oohs of the supporters. By halftime, the score was 43–20 in favor of Gentry. When the referee sounded his whistle, the players did not retreat to the locker rooms. They simply joined their respective cheerleaders on the sidelines in front of their supporters.

Then a tall, bearded, heavyset man dressed in a dark suit and cowboy boots grabbed a microphone and walked to the middle of the court. Austin noticed that his tan, almost-yellow boots contrasted sharply with his suit. His tie was also very long, almost covering his pants' zipper. In a deep and commanding voice, he said, "Good evening, folks! I'm Peter Brown, the principal here at Gentry. This is a very special night here at Gentry for two reasons. The first one is that we have the two undefeated high-school boys' basketball teams in the Delta playing for the first time this season. Have they not been awesome? Let's give them a round of applause!"

Everybody in the gymnasium got on their feet and joined in thunderous applause and seismic screaming and cheering for the teams. It took more than two minutes for Mr. Brown to resume his speech, as the excitement-fueled clapping and screaming lasted that long. "The second reason this night is so special is because we have a unique guest who has traveled more than seventeen thousand miles, all the way from Cameroon, Africa, to join our faculty here at Gentry. As a matter of fact, he just arrived here tonight, and I have not met him yet. Due to the acute shortage of foreign-language teachers in this area, we had to go all the way to a French-speaking country to find a highly qualified teacher to come and boost our foreign-language program. I will let him come to the floor and introduce himself."

Excited but extremely nervous, Austin walked to the center of the court, where the principal was standing. With a broad smile on his thick-bearded face, Mr. Brown said, "Welcome to Indianola, Mississippi, young man. We are very happy you have agreed to join our faculty here at Gentry High School."

Austin thanked him and said the honor was all his. Then he grabbed the microphone from his new boss, cleared his throat, and started speaking. There was cemetery-like silence in the gymnasium.

"Good evening! My name is Austin Annenkeng. I am from Mbengwi, Cameroon. That's in Central Africa. I am very delighted to finally make it to Indianola to begin a new phase in my career. Judging from the great excitement of the crowd and the huge turnout here tonight, I could say that you all have tremendous passion for your school. I am very pleased with the choice I made to come to Gentry High School over going to the other choice that I was presented with, in Oregon." There was a thunderous round of applause and cheers, and then the crowd got quiet again to let him continue.

"I don't know how long I am going to be here, but I am sure about one thing: I will spend every day sharing the knowledge and skills I have with the students of this great high school. Thank you very much for the warm reception, and I look forward to a productive and enjoyable time in this city. Thank you!"

Everybody got on their feet and clapped as Austin returned to his seat in the front row of the bleachers.

For the remainder of the game, Austin received all sorts of questions from inquisitive and nosy individuals, mostly females, around him. Many of the questions were about normal things one would ask someone from a place that one had never been to, but others were incredibly inappropriate for the context. For instance, one lady, probably between twenty-five and thirty years old, insisted that he answer her question about African men having very large penises and high libido. She was very beautiful and scantily dressed, leaving very little to the imagination of the beholder. Her persistence earned her a response. Austin looked around and then whispered the response in her ear. Whatever he said got her grinning and smiling. He caught her a few times thereafter staring at him, right below his belt.

A guy in his late twenties wanted to know if it was true that in Africa men could get married to more than one wife. He got a confirmation of what he had previously heard from his peers but had dismissed as just ignorant talk by promiscuous young men. "If that's true, I need to move to Africa then. Shit! I'll be balling over there!" He turned and shared what he had just learned with the friend to his right, and, before long, the word had spread to everybody on the home side of the bleachers.

After the game, the principal informed Austin that the school district had arranged for his family to host him for a few months until he got on his feet. He lived in a neighboring city, Greenville. The twenty-five-minute drive in the GMC Yukon that night was long and exhausting. He got hammered with even more questions, some of which he had already received from other inquisitive individuals that night. The questioning continued with intensity over late-night dinner when they finally got home and were joined at the table by Mrs. Brown and their fourteen-year-old son. Austin hid his tiredness well. He remained calm, courteous, and polite, even though he wished for his hosts to show him his bed and save some of the questions for the next day. He got his wish at 11:57 p.m.

The guest bedroom was in the west end of the three-bedroom house. It was well furnished and neatly arranged. The queen-sized bed had a high Serta pillow-top mattress that had just the right softness. The blue sheets matched the walls, while the soft and thick comforter seemed to have been made from the same cloth as the elegant curtains on the giant windows. There was a comfortable couch on the right side of the bed and a forty-inch TV sitting on a dresser about six feet away from the foot of the bed.

Austin shut the door and collapsed on the bed with his clothes still on. He barely had the strength to kick his shoes off. It seemed as if he had not been sleeping for an hour when there was a knock on the door followed by a deep voice announcing that they would be heading back to Indianola in an hour.

Chapter Nineteen

First Day Teaching in America

Austin sluggishly got out of bed, prayed for God's guidance and protection, and took a shower. Then he half unzipped his luggage and pulled out something to wear without unpacking, as he was running out of time. By the time he was done getting ready for work, there was only five minutes left to eat his breakfast of grits, eggs, biscuits, and milk. When he asked for sugar after tasting the grits, his hosts exchanged a look that he did not quite understand before their son passed a glass container down the table to him. His boss grabbed the rest of his breakfast to go, and Austin followed suit.

The ride to school that morning was much shorter. Mr. Brown was less curious. "Are you nervous about your first day of teaching in America?" he asked.

"No! I'm anxious and excited. I'm glad it's finally here," Austin said.

"Well, I'm grateful to you for doing this. If you need anything, just let me know. I will tell the faculty and staff to provide you with all the assistance and support you will need to do your job successfully."

His first day of teaching was very interesting. No one in his six French classes was interested in learning the language on that day. The students had all kinds of questions about Cameroon in particular and Africa in general. Some of the questions they asked included, "What is the capital of Africa? Is it true that y'all live on trees over there? Is it true that lions and zebras and other wild animals just be roaming around everywhere? Do y'all have McDonalds? What kind of food do y'all be eating over there?

Do y'all have cars? Did you buy your clothes when you got to America? I know that in Africa, y'all be running around naked." And so on.

There were also questions about the number of wives a man could marry in Cameroon and others about the genitals and libido of African men.

Austin learned about the boldness of his students on that day. Right before the bell rang at the end of first period, a female student in the first desk in the first column near the door raised her hand and asked, "Can you take me to the club on Saturday?"

The shock on her teacher's face let her know that she had crossed the line. Several of her classmates had asked inappropriate questions earlier, which Austin simply ignored, but hers had taken the inappropriateness way too far. She was saved by the bell, as Austin was getting ready to issue a stern verbal warning to her.

During change of class, a couple of students stopped by to hand a piece of paper to Austin as he stood in the hallway. They said it was from the sub in room seventeen. He asked them what a sub was, and they said it was a substitute teacher filling in for someone who was absent. There was a name and a phone number on the piece of paper. The first name was Cynthia, just like the name of the persistent lady from the previous night in the gym. He wondered if it was from her.

It didn't take long for him to get confirmation of the hand that had penned the name and digits. As he was speaking to his students and facing the wall of glass windows on the other side of the classroom, he recognized the individual waving aggressively in front of the classroom opposite his. She was determined to get his attention, regardless of the crazy looks she was getting from passing students, faculty, and staff.

Austin pretended not to have seen her, even though he was very pleased with where he saw things going. He smiled. She was clearly not dressed for the job she had been invited to do on that day, but that was above his pay grade. Evidently, she was determined to get concrete confirmation of the theory about African males' penises and libido. The way she looked, he would not under any circumstances hesitate to grant her wish.

Four other classes came after the second period, but Austin was surprised by the similarity in student behavior from one class to the next. They asked the same questions, were equally bold and disruptive, did not seem to care if they got to class late, talked back to the teacher, and treated school property (textbooks, computers, desks, tables, chairs, etc.) with so much disrespect. At the end of the day, his neighbor next door told him that she had written up twelve students that day and had called for an administrator to remove a student from her room twice before lunch. Then she asked him about school policies regarding student misbehavior in Cameroon.

He told her that in Cameroon, the students were definitely not saints, but the teachers, especially those in public schools, had a lot of power in dealing with student misbehavior. They could kick a disrespectful student out of class for as long as they wanted. They could prevent a student from coming to class until they had bought all the books and other required class materials. They could fail a child if they needed to without the principal's approval. "With that much power in the hands of the teachers, the students come to class prepared to learn and to avoid anything that might make the teacher mad," he said. Then he added, "In Cameroon there is a common saying that after God there is the teacher."

He cited several instances when he put his teacher's needs over his parents', including the day in middle school when his father sent him to the neighborhood store to buy a packet of cigarettes. When he got there, his math teacher told him to take some groceries to his wife on the other side of the town. He took care of his teacher's errand before returning to the store to get what his father wanted. When he returned home, his father was very upset, as he had been waiting for his cigarettes for over two hours. But when Austin told him why it had taken him so long to return with the cigarettes, he shook his head in understanding and said, "Oh! That's not a problem at all. You should have told me that as soon as you came in."

The art teacher listened attentively to Austin as he described school-disciplinary procedures and issues in Cameroon, and when he was done, she told him, "Welcome to America. Brace yourself! The students are tougher to handle here, and the principals themselves are sometimes unable to handle disciplinary problems firmly and effectively because their hands are tied." Austin did not understand what she meant by the principals' hands being tied, but she had to take the referrals to the main office before it closed.

While Austin was waiting in his classroom for his ride home with his boss, he reflected on his performance on his first day on the job. He concluded that if he was going to be successful, he would need strong classroom management, high expectations for his students, clear and effective classroom procedures and routines, and fair and consistent classroom rules and consequences. He also needed to come up with a plan to deal with Cynthia and the likes of her before things got out of control. He had heard and read about women in America being very bold and aggressive in making moves to get the man they wanted, but he had often thought that the details of the stories were a little exaggerated. Evidently they were not.

Even though school got out at 3:00 p.m., it wasn't until 5:30 p.m. that Austin's principal and host was ready to head back to Greenville.

"So, Austin, how was your first day?"

"It was productive. I spent most of the time answering my students' questions about Cameroon and Africa. I was also able to discuss with them the plan for the rest of the semester, the supplies they would need, my expectations, and class rules. However, I will need to emphasize the expectations, rules, and classroom procedures as often as needed, because I learned today that the classes might be difficult to manage."

"Yes, classroom management could pose a problem if you do not have clear student expectations, firm class rules, and simple procedures that you implement consistently and fairly. If you need help with any of these, let me know. I have already instructed the assistant principal and the guidance counselors to give you all the assistance you need. The teachers also know that they have to help you, since you are not from here, and you are starting in the middle of the school year."

"Thank you very much, sir. Based on what I saw and dealt with today, I will need all of that help."

"What exactly did you deal with? The students were not all that bad, were they?"

Austin described the behavior issues that he had had to handle but added that his students left mostly a positive impression on him the first day. In his narrative of his day, he deliberately left out the details about the lady who sent him a note with her phone number through a couple of students.

They got home around 6:05 p.m. After dinner, where Austin had to repeat all the information he had shared with his boss on their way to Greenville, he unpacked his luggage, took a shower, prayed, and went to bed a few minutes before 10:00 p.m. Thus ended his first day as a teacher in the United States.

Chapter Twenty

Living with a Host Family

Austin lived with the Browns for the entire second semester, from January to May 2004. He liked to help his host mother in the kitchen to prepare meals, clean dishes, set the table, and clear it after meals. Whenever he was around her, she was always interested in learning more about Cameroon and Africa, and Austin did not mind sharing everything he knew, even though some of her questions were reruns from days or weeks earlier. She was an exceptionally kind woman, and she treated Austin as her own son. The least he could do to show gratitude was quench her thirst for knowledge about his country and continent of origin and to help her with household chores.

Mrs. Brown was a high-school English teacher in a neighboring town. She was dark skinned and about five five. She had an average body build and average-length dreadlocks. She often wore glasses to alleviate her failing sight. Austin never asked her how old she was, but he suspected that she was probably in her fifties. She hailed originally from Louisiana but had moved to Mississippi, the home state of her husband, after stays in Florida and Alabama. How they had met was unknown to Austin, but they had been married for more than twenty years. She was soft spoken, thoughtful, and very opinionated. Austin often wondered if she was at all religious, because she never went with him, her husband, and her son to church on Sundays.

Mr. Brown was Baptist, but he never took Austin to the same church twice in the five months that he spent with his family. The very first time, they went to a Baptist church off Highway 61 in Cleveland, Mississippi. After three hours, the preacher didn't give signs that the service would be ending soon. That was exceptionally torturous for Austin, who was used to the hour-long service of the Catholic church he had gone to his entire life. When the service finally ended, the pastor asked if there were any visitors, and Mr. Brown got up and said, "Reverend, I have a special guest with me who is visiting us all the way from Africa. He is a teacher at my school, and we are very happy with the work he is doing with our students."

Everybody in the congregation turned to see who the special guest was, but the pastor was not content with just looking at Austin from the pulpit. He asked him to come to the pulpit and introduce himself. With hundreds of eyes watching and scanning him from head to toe, Austin nervously walked to the front and introduced himself. When he thought he was done and was about to return to his seat, an old lady in the front row asked what his name was again. Then her neighbor asked him for the spelling. That opened the floodgates for what seemed like hundreds of questions that took a little over an hour to respond to. They were all questions that he had already answered a million times for other people at different locations.

The next Sunday, Mr. Brown took Austin to a different church in Indianola, but things played out just like the previous Sunday. There was a very long service followed by a request by the pastor for visitors to stand up to be recognized and Austin's host father stating that he had a special guest with him and the preacher handing Austin the microphone to answer questions that he had heard so many times that he could even offer a response before someone could finish asking his or her question. When church was finally over, Mr. Brown, in his usual Sunday routine, went by his office at the school and stayed there for several hours, leaving Austin and his teenage son to wait in the truck until he came out.

By mid-February, Austin was starting to hate Sundays because of the thought of what he knew he would have to endure if he went to church with his host. Thus, he started feigning sickness on Saturday evening to get out of going to church the next day.

Nevertheless, there was one activity that Austin really enjoyed doing on weekends with his host dad. On many Saturdays, they would get up early to do yard work, and after that, they would eat breakfast that was prepared by Mrs. Brown. On some occasions, Mr. Brown would take the guys to Dunkin' Donuts for breakfast. Even though Austin liked the home meals, he enjoyed having the delicious doughnuts and coffee after a few hours of yard work on a Saturday.

Whenever he had free time and his host parents did not need him to help with something, Austin spent time in his room watching television, reading, surfing the Internet, and talking on the telephone. Since he didn't have a car, he couldn't go anywhere. Cynthia had picked him up a few times to spend time at a hotel, but he didn't want his boss to find out that they knew each other, or, much worse, that she was picking him up at his residence.

At least six other girls, including the art teacher next to his classroom, came by on different occasions to pick him up surreptitiously, and they would hurriedly go make out at a hotel or in the car deep in the country. He was finding it challenging to resist the advances of the ladies every-where he went. Living with a host family helped him control that to an extent, although from time to time, a persistent female such as Cynthia wanted to be introduced to the host family so that she could see Austin easily and frequently.

When he wanted to clear his head, he would go for a walk down Irish Lane and to the park. One Friday evening, as he left to go for a walk, he was stopped by five police officers about a hundred feet from the house. There had been a robbery in the neighborhood, and the perpetra-tor was still in the vicinity. A sea of blue lights was coming from eight or ten cruisers, and the whole scenario frightened Austin, who had never been stopped by the police before, either in Cameroon or in the United States. The officers asked him for an ID, but he didn't have it on him. He told them that he lived next door and that he didn't think he needed one to go for a walk down the street.

Things got tense when the officers, who were all white, noticed his accent. They asked him where he was from, what he was doing in the city, how long he had been there, if he had authorization to be in the United States, and so on. They even asked the white homeowner whose house had been burglarized if he had even seen Austin in the neighborhood, and he said he did not recognize him. With his entire body and voice trembling, Austin pleaded for the cops to go with him to the house so that he could show them proof of everything he was telling them, but they would not have it. They were about to cuff him and hurl him into one of the cruisers when another officer, a black one, came and asked them if they had apprehended the suspect. They told him what had happened, and he said they could at least verify whether Austin was telling the truth or not.

So, surrounded by six cops, Austin was accompanied home, but when he could not open the door because he had forgotten to take his key with him, one of them said, "I knew he was feeding us a bunch of bullshit." At that point, Austin clenched his fist and pounded on the door with all his strength. The three occupants of the house rushed to the window and pulled the curtains to see who or what was at the door. When they saw Austin in the midst of the cops, one of them opened the door.

"What's going on, officers?" the lady of the house asked.

"Does this individual live here?" one of them asked.

"Yes, he is our guest. We are his host family. He is a visiting teacher at Gentry High School in Indianola. He left the house about fifteen minutes ago to go for a walk, like he often does around this time. What did he do?" Brown asked.

"We just stopped him because there has been a robbery in the area, and since he couldn't produce any identification documents, we decided to look a little deeper. Could we see his papers?" another officer said.

Austin went to his room and brought back his passport with his J-1 visa, which was valid. He also showed them his exchange-teacher ID from Amity Institute. The officers apologized for the inconvenience, but Austin's host parents were not satisfied. They were very angry and let the officers know that had Austin been white, he would not have been stopped. They told the officers that the matter was not over.

The next afternoon, as Austin was packing up some papers to grade over the weekend, the school secretary buzzed his classroom to inform him that the superintendent wanted to see him at the district office. She had sent her driver to pick him up. Wondering what the meeting was for, he immediately left for the district office.

When he got there, the superintendent apologized for the incident with Greenville police the night before, as if she were responsible for it. She was concerned that the encounter might have left a bitter taste in Austin's mouth and that he might not want to return to the Mississippi Delta after the school year was over. She told him that she had expressed her disgust to the police chief and that the latter had apologized, but she had insisted that he apologize directly to him. "Therefore, we are going to Greenville to meet with him," she said.

They met the police chief in his office later that afternoon. He said he was sorry that his men had acted the way they had. He also advised Austin to always carry an ID with him in case of an emergency. After the meeting at the police station, Austin's superintendent treated him to a sumptuous dinner at Garfield's, a restaurant in the Greenville Mall.

The following day, Mrs. Brown asked Austin if he would like to ride to Senatobia to watch her son's soccer game. Since he had no specific plans for the weekend, he did not turn down the offer. It would be a great distraction from thoughts about a crazy week.

The Browns' fourteen-year-old son was a spectacular athlete. He excelled in multiple team and individual sports, including soccer, football, basketball, baseball, track and field, judo, karate, and tennis. He was following in the footsteps of his father. His dad had played football, basketball, and baseball in high school and college before starting his professional career as a college football coach. He eventually coached high-school football and basketball. Even while he worked as a school administrator, he still served part-time as a referee for high-school basketball and football games. He was very proud that his son, Pete, was replicating his talents, and he did his best to go to as many of his games as possible to cheer him on, including the soccer game in Senatobia.

With their restless, excited, and resolutely supportive parents and well-wishers cheering them on the sidelines, Pete's team went on to defeat their opponents by a score of 3–0. They earned their victory by dominating the other team for the entire ninety minutes. The defeat could have been much worse had it not been for a few narrow misses by the team captain.

After the game, Mr. Brown took his family to a Mexican restaurant in Cleveland, Mississippi, to celebrate the victory. Austin had his first taste of Mexican cuisine on that day. He ordered a plate of carnitas and found it to be very delicious. He was going to try it again whenever the opportunity presented itself.

At 5:23 p.m., Mrs. Brown's Jeep Cherokee truck slowly came to a stop in their driveway. It had been a long and exhausting day, and Austin was looking forward to spending the rest of the evening watching television in bed. He sluggishly got out of the car, and without paying attention to what he was doing, he slammed the door with his right hand while supporting himself by placing his left hand on what he thought was the roof of the car, right above the door. Unfortunately for him, the closing door caught half of his left thumb, and the excruciating pain brought him back to complete consciousness.

It didn't take long for the finger to turn red, then purple, and finally black. It also doubled in size within an hour. At Austin's insisting, Mrs. Brown drove him to the emergency room at King's Daughters Hospital, a few miles from the house. He was in tremendous pain as they waited for three hours before a nurse came and insisted on completing a stack of paper work and other preliminary things that she said had to be done before he could be seen by the doctor. All that took an additional forty-five minutes. While they waited, Austin kept wondering what would have happened if he had something more severe, such as a heart attack, or if he had been in a ghastly car accident.

The wait was unbearable. At one point he walked out of the room to read the sign on the wall to ensure that they had not gone to a regular consultation room. They were at the right place, the emergency room, and he had a real emergency, but the wait was longer than what he had seen at hospitals in Cameroon, where patients waited in line for hours to see a doctor. But he was not in Africa. He was in the United States, where the hospitals were supposed to be the best in the world in terms of both the quality and the speed of the care.

When he was finally seen by a doctor, the care didn't last more than twenty minutes. The physician used a needle to drill a tiny hole in Austin's nail to release the pressure. A pink liquid oozed out of it for several seconds, and then he wrapped the finger in a bandage, and that was it. Twenty minutes, and that was it, but a few weeks later, Austin received a bill for $2,755 after his insurance had taken care of their part. He could not believe that the hospital was billing him that much for what clearly was substandard and underneath-emergency-room-quality service. However, he was not going to let depressing thoughts about the ER and the ridiculous bill ruin his upcoming spring break.

School got out for a week in the middle of March 2004. Apart from touring the Delta; traveling to Amory, Mississippi, the hometown of Mr. Brown; and reading, Austin spent a lot of time with his colleague, Mary, the art teacher. She often picked him up, stealthily, to go to different Mexican restaurants, his favorite. On one occasion, they went to one off Highway 81 in Greenville. While they were eating, Mary told him that a group of guys at the table across from theirs were staring incessantly at them, and it was making her uncomfortable. She also told him not to turn around to look at the guys. He heeded her warning, but when he left minutes later to relieve himself, the guys followed.

They accosted him in the restroom as he was washing his hands. One of them stood on each side of him and three behind him, completely blocking his way. He calmly turned around and asked them what their problem was. They did not respond. They just stood there, probably waiting for him to attempt to force his way out of the bathroom. He didn't have to, because barely seconds later, a man brought his son in to use the restroom, and they disrupted whatever the five white males in their twenties were about to do to Austin.

He returned to Mary, who was beyond worried that he had been gone for too long, especially as she had seen the five fellows follow him to the bathroom. He told her that the guys had accosted him in the restroom, but she didn't seem too surprised. She said that in the Mississippi Delta, interracial dating was commonly frowned upon and that at times, couples would get attacked by disapproving white people. They even had names for whites who committed the crime of dating a black person, such as "nigger lover" and "white trash." Mary apologized for not warning Austin earlier. She also said that in the future, they would head to a larger city, like Jackson, to hang out. She had heard that people were more tolerant of interracial dating there.

After spring break, the rest of the school year ran out pretty fast. In the midst of end-of-year exams, award programs, graduation, and other end-of-school-year activities, Austin had to make arrangements for a place to stay and a means of transportation when school resumed in the fall. His stay at the Browns was going to expire once school got out.

He looked around Indianola for a decent apartment to rent, but he didn't find any. His active search for his own place was much to the chagrin of Mary and the other ladies he had known, because they were willing to do anything to have him move in with them. Knowing how dangerous such propositions were and how much his freedom was important to him, he turned down all the offers without hesitation. One of the ladies' offers was the type that was difficult to refuse. She wanted him to move into her beautiful house in one of the best neighborhoods in Indianola. He would not need to pay a dime for anything and would also be using one of her three cars, a Lexus LS 400. "I appreciate the very generous offer, but I prefer to get my own place. You would be welcome there, and our relationship is not going to change," he told her.

He had not found an apartment he liked by the time of his return flight to Cameroon on May 26, 2004. Therefore, he decided to continue the search on his return in July. He flew to Cameroon out of Memphis International Airport via Houston and Amsterdam on KLM flights.

His family was happy to have him back home for a short stay. His father's condition was still serious but stable. His days in Cameroon were incredibly busy, as he had to meet with his dissertation advisor to assess the progress he had made on his research while in the United States. He also visited his siblings in Buea and Yaoundé, his grandmother in Dchang, and his friends in Bamenda and Douala. Additionally, he had to apply for an extension of his J-1 visa. His relationship with Era, which had been put on hold for five months, also received a significant jolt during that time, but by the time it got to the climax, the Atlantic Ocean flowed in, separating them once again. He left Cameroon for Mississippi on July 27, 2004.

Chapter Twenty-One

Getting an Apartment and a Car

Upon his return to the Mississippi Delta, Austin stayed with a friend, a fellow African, from Senegal, while he continued his search for his own apartment and a means of transportation. The search for the latter was a top priority, as he thought it would facilitate the quest for the former. So he went to car dealerships in Cleveland, Greenville, and Indianola to find a dependable and reliable car. But everywhere he went, he was turned down for financing. At the GM dealership in Greenville, he was told he could not get financing for the Toyota Camry he liked because he did not have any credit.

"How can I get credit?" he asked the manager.

"To get credit in America, you have to buy something on credit," the manager said.

"But that's exactly what I am trying to do. I want this Camry on credit."

"I'm sorry; we can't sell you this car on credit, because you don't have any credit. In this country you have to have credit to buy things on credit, and you have to pay for them on time monthly to build your credit and to become more creditworthy. When I pull your credit, I don't see any evidence that you have ever purchased anything on credit. You don't have any credit at all. It's like you're a brand-new baby. You're more than twenty-five years old, and you don't have any credit?"

"That's because I was not born in the United States. I just moved here. I have a good job, and I will be able to make the monthly payments on time." Austin's frustration was getting palpable.

"We can't give you the Camry on credit, but there's another car that we can sell to someone without any credit."

The manager took Austin past all the new cars out front and proceeded beyond the far end of the lot, where all the used cars were. Then he turned left and headed toward a beauty shop in another building. Sandwiched between the beauty shop and the dealership's auto-repair garage was an old maroon Mercury Grand Marquis. It looked as if it had been sitting there, forgotten, for a very long time.

"I'll let you have this baby right here on credit for only five thousand dollars with a one-thousand-dollar down payment," the manager told Austin with great excitement, as if he were doing him a huge favor.

"Thank you for the offer, but that's not the kind of car I'm looking for."

"Nobody's going to give you the kind of car you're looking for on credit, because you don't have any credit!"

Austin thanked the manager once more for his time and left the dealership, depressed, frustrated, and confused. "They want me to buy something on credit in order to get credit, but they'll not sell me a car on credit, even though I have a very good job and a salary, and I can make the monthly payments easily. This does not make any damn sense," he thought.

The next day, his Senegalese friend took him to a used-car lot in Moorhead, Mississippi, to see if the owner would give him a chance to own a car "without any credit." To Austin's surprise, the credit conditions were less stringent there. The only thing that the owner of the business needed was proof of a stable job and a steady income, and Austin fit both criteria perfectly. A down payment was not required, but it was encouraged.

He was given a 2000 Toyota Camry with a full tank of gas to try for forty-eight hours, and if he was satisfied with it, it would be his after all the paper work was drawn up and signed. He didn't need that long to test-drive the car. After work the next day, he returned to the dealership to sign the required documents and pay a $500 down payment to keep the car. It would cost him $5,000, and his monthly car note was $200.

Possessing his own car made looking for a place to stay much easier. He didn't have to plead with the few people he knew to take him around to find an apartment to rent, especially as the people he knew were busy professionals. A colleague of his called him less than a week after he bought his car to tell him that there was an apartment for rent on Baker Street in Indianola. He called the number and made arrangements to see the place after work the next day.

The place was a two-bedroom apartment on the second floor of a building facing Highway 82. It had a large kitchen and a dining room. The walls of the entire apartment were made of wood panels. New carpeting had been installed in all the rooms except the kitchen and the single bathroom, where there were newly installed vinyl floors. The landlord used the first floor as storage for supplies for other rental properties he had in and around Indianola.

The gray building was behind another house of similar color, also owned by the same landlord. The house in front was 303 Baker Street, while the vacant apartment was 303½ Baker Street. It was the perfect spot for a bachelor. He liked the view of the highway. There was a shopping center across the road with several businesses, including a restaurant, a medical-supplies store, a beauty shop, a barbershop, and an insurance agency. To the left and right of the single-apartment building were two single-family homes, one on each side. The monthly rent for the apartment was $300, and the landlord needed the same amount as deposit and the first month's rent before issuing a one-year lease. Austin fulfilled the requirements on the spot and took possession of the keys.

Keys in hand, Austin went furniture hunting. He was in a hurry to move into his own place. Sleeping on his friend's couch as he had been doing was keeping him constantly tired, and it was very difficult to be an effective teacher without getting enough sleep at night. All he needed for a start was a bed—nothing fancy—a mattress, a pillow, and something to cover his body at night. The rest would come later, progressively.

However, if he thought that it would be easier to get financing for the pieces he needed since they did not cost much, he was dead wrong.

Everywhere he went, he was turned down for lack of credit, even though he was told that he needed to purchase something on credit in order to get credit. That was when one of his ladies, Cynthia, offered to let him have one of her beds with bedding included. But he turned down the tempting offer due to the obvious strings he knew were attached to it. He also thought that it would not be an honorable thing to do.

Thus, he endured the pain of sleeping on the couch and hearing his friend having sex loudly all night, Monday through Sunday, in his bedroom, often without even shutting the door. That would not have mattered anyway, because the walls of his dirt-cheap one-bedroom apartment were as thin as loose-leaf paper. After two more days, he couldn't take it anymore. He decided to try one last furniture store in Indianola that he had been avoiding because he had been told that the owners would provide financing to anyone, even a madman off the streets, with few to no restrictions but at ridiculously high interest rates.

He got a bed and a mattress from there and vowed to pay them off within a month or two to cut the interest. He also purchased two pillows, a blanket, and bedsheets at Walmart and excitedly moved into his apartment. The place was empty, but he was thrilled to have his own roof over his head.

Austin's exhilaration was boosted the following day when he was informed that he was being moved to the junior high school, where there was a high need for a teacher with his unique qualification to teach French and English. That was great for him for two reasons: the junior high school was just three minutes down the street from his apartment, and the class sizes there as well as the faculty were a lot smaller. His students at the high school were taken over by another French teacher. The school year was starting off pretty well for him, and he was determined to keep things that way.

Chapter Twenty-Two

Alone in Rural Mississippi

Austin moved into his apartment on September 1, 2004, and that gave him some much-needed peace of mind to focus on his career and work on his PhD thesis. Although he had been spending some time on the latter, his mind wasn't settled enough to give it the attention it needed. So he decided to spend at least an hour on it every day, no matter what happened. Since he didn't have the appropriate furniture at home to do that, he had to stay after school on weekdays to write his thesis, and on weekends, he wrote on the carpet in his empty living room, or he went to the Indianola city library.

By December that year, he was done writing, and he took the almost-four-hundred-page draft thesis to Office Depot in Greenville to print five copies, one for each of his thesis-committee members. After the printing, he put each copy together using a spiral. He then took the copies to UPS to mail them to his committee chair in Cameroon. The printing, binding, and mailing cost him over $1,000, money he could have used to purchase some highly needed furniture and kitchen utensils for his apartment, but he firmly believed that the short-term suffering would yield significant long-term benefits.

Speaking of temporary pain, Austin also deprived himself of any fun while he was producing his thesis, but once it was completed and mailed, he started hanging out with colleagues and going on dates, especially as schools had closed for Christmas. His friend Cynthia offered to bring groceries over to his apartment to cook Christmas dinner for him, and he accepted without much thought. That was a terrible mistake, because it made her think that she was the lady of the house. She started leaving clothes and other personal items there, which became increasingly difficult for Austin to hide rapidly if he brought some other lady home.

On December 31, 2004, what he had long dreaded happened. His other girlfriend, Marie, stopped by without calling ahead of time, and Austin was at home with Cynthia, who had arrived earlier to spend the last day of the year with him. When he heard the knock on the door, he knew something was wrong, because he was not expecting anyone. He rushed to the kitchen window and slightly pulled the blinds to peep out at his driveway to see if he could recognize the car of the person at his door.

Parked in his driveway, right behind Cynthia's Mercedes, was a familiar silver Lexus sedan. He returned to his bedroom and placed his right index finger on his mouth, signaling to Cynthia to be quiet. Then the knocks on the door became very loud poundings, followed by "Open the fucking door, Austin! I know you're in there. Your car is in the driveway. Who are you with in there?"

Things got quiet for about five minutes, and then he heard something hit the bedroom window. Since she couldn't reach the second-floor bedroom window, Marie started throwing everything she could find in the yard at it, eventually shattering the glass. At that point, Austin decided to call the police because he was afraid of what could happen next. He was being threatened from outside the apartment—and from within, as Cynthia, who had for some time been assuming that she was his one and only, or at least the lady of the house, realized that she was neither of those, and she started interrogating him, giving him hell.

"Who is that bitch out there? What does she want? How long have you been fucking her?" The questions were dropping like hail, hitting him everywhere, and he didn't even have a chance to respond. He couldn't respond even if he wanted to. He just didn't have the presence of mind for that. Everything was happening incredibly fast, and it was beginning to make him feel dizzy.

Because he wouldn't answer the questions, Cynthia looked out the broken window and immediately recognized the person who had been pounding on the door. It was someone she knew very well. Small rural town! Everybody knew one another, and Austin naïvely had not thought about that.

He was very lucky that the police got there less than five minutes after the call was made, because, after recognizing her rival, Cynthia had started throwing all kinds of insults at her through the broken window, and Marie was threatening to ramp things up a notch by turning the cars in Austin's driveway into a New Year's Eve fireworks show. The police officers immediately understood what they were dealing with, and they asked Austin if he wanted to press charges on her for the window and other damages. He said he just wanted them to escort both ladies far away from his place. He would pay the property manager to replace the window. He was thankful for the situation being defused before it spiraled out of control.

He mostly stayed indoors during the remaining three days of his Christmas break, due to embarrassment and fear of repercussions. Since moving into the apartment, he had been keeping a low profile, but the drama with the ladies made him feel as if the neighbors would have a negative impression of him. Furthermore, he had heard that American women were particularly vicious and violent when cheated on or shunned, and in a small town like Indianola, where everybody knew one another, he knew that news about the incident at his place was spreading like wildfire, and that was making him nervous.

However, the one time that he did come out to get water from the trunk of his car, the day before school resumed, the old couple who lived in the house to the left of his building greeted him and asked if he was OK. They said that they had not seen him in three days and that they were getting pretty concerned about his safety. "Why would they be concerned about my safety when I have never met or spoken to them since I moved to this neighborhood?" he thought.

They also told him that they had plenty of leftover food from their elaborate New Year celebration and offered him some, but he told them that he had already eaten. At the insistence of the lady, he accepted a piece of cake, and, to his chagrin, that just opened the door to a litany of questions about his accent, origin, family, likes, dislikes, education, career, income, the drama at his apartment a few days earlier, and so on. If he had not lied to them that he had left the iron on and he was afraid it could start a fire, they would have inundated him with further questions. They probably would have asked him if he peed standing or sitting.

They still did not let him leave without Mrs. Cooper giving him advice about American women. "Austin, you have to watch out for these women now. When they see a nice, smart, professional, and successful young man like you, they will follow you like flies following a carcass. There is an acute shortage of good black men in this country, especially in this area. The vast majority of men are either in jail or don't want to do anything with their lives. They're just looking for a woman to take care of them while they play video games, roam the streets, sell and use drugs, pop babies left and right with multiple women, and so on. I hope you wear a condom whenever you sleep with these women, because you don't want to get trapped into something you were not looking for. The girls around here would trap you with a pregnancy to force you to marry them or at least to put you on child support. Watch out, Austin! You're the dream man for these women."

When Austin finally left Mr. and Mrs. Cooper, his head was spinning from the questioning and warning about the women in the area. The latter made him borderline paranoid, and he resolved to be more cautious and perhaps avoid women all together, at least until he understood the environment better. One thing did seem clear to him, though: if he was going to see another lady, she had to live out of town, preferably in another state. That way, they would see each other when they needed to, and the rest of the time, they would focus on their jobs and whatever else they had going on.

School resumed for the second semester, and it was a welcome distraction for Austin, who had been spending too much time pondering the events of the previous week, his safety, and how to answer questions about the embarrassing encounter between the two ladies at his apartment (he was certain that the whole town would hear about it given the speed at which juicy news spreads in small towns). Contrary to his suspicions, nobody asked him about the traffic jam at his place over the Christmas break. He overheard the librarian murmur something about it to the counselor as he was walking to the cafeteria during lunch, but he ignored them and kept walking. If no one asked him about it, he wasn't going to say anything about it. Focusing only on his job enabled him to have a very productive week. His students were showing great enthusiasm and motivation to learn French and English. As a result, he started offering before- and after-school remediation and enrichment to enhance student learning and achievement.

However, dedicating his time to his job did not stop the two ladies from blowing his phone up with calls and texts to ask for an explanation and to seek to meet to talk. It did not prevent other women from casting their nets at him either. He resisted the temptation for several weeks until one cold winter evening in February, when the lights went out for hours and turned his apartment into a cold chamber. He called a lady who had subbed at his school and had obtained his number through a source that she was unwilling to unveil.

"Hey, Cheryl, how are you?" he asked charmingly.

"I'm wonderful, Austin! What a pleasant surprise! I wasn't sure if I was ever going to hear from you, since you were not happy that I obtained your number without permission and sent you a text message. Once again, I apologize for that."

"That's OK. I understand. What are you doing tonight?"

"I wanted to go to Club Ebony, but I wonder if they would be open since the entire city is in the dark tonight. How about you? What are you doing?"

"Well, I don't have anything planned yet, unless you want to come over for some wine and cheese."

"That sounds great. Let me freshen up, and I'll be on my way. I already know where you live, so I don't need directions."

Austin was going to ask her how she had gotten his address, but he quickly dropped it after realizing that if she was able to get his phone number without his permission, it was certainly possible for her to obtain his address as well. She could have also followed him one day without him noticing.

"Awesome! I will see you in a few."

She knocked on his door about an hour later. She was dressed in a very short black dress that left most of her shoulders and immense bosom exposed. She could have easily frozen that night if it weren't for the black coat that she wore over her tight, glove-like dress. She also had black, high-heeled shoes to match her dress and coat. Austin helped her get rid of the latter before they sat on his newly acquired couch in the living room, which was dimly lit by a candle on the coffee table. The lights had not returned, and he no longer missed them.

As soon as they sat down, he opened a bottle of Cabernet Sauvignon and poured a glass for her and one for himself. He picked up a piece of Laughing Cow cheese from a saucer on the coffee table and gave it to her. She had never had cheese with wine before. One bite and one sip, and she fell in love with the combination. The more wine they drank, the less the space was between them on the couch, until they were shoulder to shoulder.

At that point, there was sudden silence in the room for about five minutes. He was thinking about what to do, while she was wondering when he was going to engage what was on her mind. "Obviously he doesn't think that I came here dressed like this on such a terribly cold night just to drink his fine wine and eat some Swiss cheese," she was thinking.

Finally, with his left hand, he gently took her right hand and gave it a few soft caresses before going up her arm and further on to her naked shoulders. At that point, she pounced on him like a tigress in heat. The couch eventually ran out of space for them, and they took the party to the bedroom. She spent the night at his place, and when she left in the morning, he was mad at himself for giving in to the temptation to do something that he had vowed to avoid. He concluded that he was just human, and the night was too cold for a young man to spend alone, with all the women who were virtually sexually harassing him everywhere he turned.

The rest of that winter, he relapsed even further. It was as if he had a beauty pageant at his apartment when he wasn't at work. Women came and went daily, sometimes two or three within twenty-four hours, especially on weekends. He had his lucky stars to thank, for those women never met one another at his place. He also did one thing differently: he told each one of them up front that he wasn't looking for a relationship. However, that didn't stop some of them from wanting more than fun after being with him a couple of times.

He slowed down during the first week of May when he received feedback from all of his doctoral thesis-committee members, and he began to spend his time after work on making the corrections that were suggested. He needed to get everything done and have the second draft ready before school got out for the summer. He dedicated two hours to the thesis every day, regardless of his daily school and weekend schedule and activities. That was how he was able to finish the corrections and mail copies of the second draft to his committee members in Cameroon. He decided to wait for feedback in the United States. That meant spending the entire summer break, from May 28 to August 8, in the United States, and without any other important tasks to keep him productively occupied, Austin had to look for ways to spend his days out of school.

Chapter Twenty-Three

Idle in the Delta

They say in Cameroon that an idle mind is the devil's workshop. That adage caught up with Austin that summer. He found out through a friend in Atlanta that there was a huge Cameroonian community in Memphis, Tennessee, and that the group had a general assembly meeting on the first Saturday of every month. He obtained enough details to attend the next meeting on the first Saturday in June.

He drove for two and a half hours to get to the gathering at the home of the president of the association. When he arrived at 7:00 p.m., things were already in motion. He was warmly received and introduced to the community as a Cameroonian brother living in Mississippi. He asked about the requirements for membership and immediately paid all the required fees and dues to join.

After that, he cut loose and started checking out the ladies. He spotted one who looked half white and half black, and she instantly became his target. There was a guy sitting right next to her, to her right. He seemed to be saying something important to her in the midst of the loud music, but whatever it was, she didn't seem to be interested, and she looked desperately in need of someone to rescue her. Austin noticed it and walked over and asked her to dance with him. She did not hesitate.

They danced to a couple of songs by Petit-Pays while talking.

"I've not been able to keep my eyes off you since I walked in here. You're outstandingly pretty! What's your name?" he asked.

"Thank you! My name is Judith," she said. Then she added, "I've been coming to this meeting for several years, but I don't recall ever seeing you."

"You're right. This is my first time attending, and it looks like I picked the best night to come, because I have met you. I would like to get to know you. I live in Indianola, Mississippi. I'm a teacher out there. What do you do for a living?"

"I'm a pediatrician. It's a pleasure meeting you," she said.

Judging from her response, Austin concluded that she was into him, so he asked, "May I have your number?"

"I can't give you my number, but give your number to Timmy, the host of this event, and I'll get it from him to call you later."

Austin viewed that as a polite but complicated way to dismiss him, yet he kept his cool till the end of the song before leaving her and vanishing into the crowd.

He spent three more hours at the gathering of the members of the Cameroonian community living in the mid-South, including Tennessee, Mississippi, and Arkansas. He also had the opportunity to eat some Cameroonian food, such as eru, achu, ndole, koki and fufu, and njama njama. He had not eaten any of those in more than a year. He was like a kid in a candy store. He told the host that he felt as if he were in Cameroon because of the ambience and the cuisine. There were even some popular Cameroonian drinks, such as 33 Export, Beaufort, Mutzig, and Satzenbrau. All the drinks and the food had been shipped from home for the event. By the time he was ready to drive home, he was drunk and sluggish, but he would not listen to the pleas of the host to spend the night and travel the next day.

He drove slowly with the windows down to let the breeze blow into his face, to keep him awake and as alert as possible. The normally two-hour drive took him three and a half hours. He went straight to bed upon arriving home, without any incidents, a bit after 3:00 a.m.

The next day he woke up around noon and took a long bath. After that, he looked in his refrigerator for something to eat. There were three carryout boxes, and he could not tell how they had gotten there. When he opened the first one and saw the ndole, his memory started coming back. The host of the event had given him some food to take home since he was single and had not eaten any Cameroonian food in more than a year.

Austin was very happy with this discovery, and he quickly heated up some ndole and plantains and poured a glass of Cabernet Sauvignon and sat down for lunch. Back in his undergrad days in Yaoundé, his friends and he had discovered that the best medication for a hangover was even more alcohol and food. The remedy did not fail, and after lunch, he sat on the couch and watched television for a while.

He thought about what to do for the rest of his summer break but couldn't come up with much. He wished his committee members would finish their review of his dissertation and send their feedback in a timely manner, but that was pure wishful thinking. Those guys were reputed for prioritizing everything else except their job. It would be a long time before he would hear from them. With two months left before he would return to work and having nothing constructive to do or the deep pockets to take trips and do other fun things, Austin resorted to what he knew best, drinking and getting in trouble with women. He met new ones and hooked up with old ones.

Exactly three weeks after the Cameroonians of the mid-South meeting in Memphis, his phone rang late one night, and there was a lady on the other end of the line. She said her name was Judith, and she asked if he remembered her. He pretended not to, and she had to help him.

"We met a few weeks ago at the African party in Memphis. I'm the girl you spoke to."

"I spoke to many people that night."

"You asked me for my number, and I told you to give yours to Timmy. I told you I was a pediatrician. Do you remember now?"

"I do. I thought that I would never hear from you since you didn't take my number or give me yours."

"Well, you were mistaken! Anyway, it was a pleasure meeting you that night. I've been thinking about you."

"I'm sorry I can't say the same because of the way things went when we met, but I'm happy you called."

She ignored the last remark and changed the subject to what Austin was doing with his time off that summer. He lied. He said he had already read nine books and had several more to go. He said that he was also spending time doing research for his doctoral dissertation. They spent almost two hours on the phone that night, and by the time they got off, she was hooked. She was impressed. She thought that he was like no man she knew. She promised to take off work to visit him in Indianola the following day, Monday.

She arrived a little after lunchtime on that day. They sat on the couch quietly for what seemed like forever, and then she asked, "What have you been doing today?"

"I've been reading Dan Brown's *The Da Vinci Code*."

"I've heard about it. Isn't there a movie with the same title? What's the book about?"

He summarized the first five chapters. She got closer to him at every word that came out of his mouth.

"I just love your accent. It's so sexy!" she said.

She didn't let him finish the summary, as before he could realize it, she was already kissing him more fiercely than any lady had before. He pretended to put up a resistance, but it was no match against her persistence. They eventually took the play to the bedroom, and by the time they were done, three hours later, they were both starving and parched. Austin served some Cabernet Sauvignon while giving her a list of the restaurants in the area. Then they took a bath together and drove to the Garfield's in Greenville.

Judith's twenty-four-hour stay with Austin was so amazing that she was back in Indianola on Friday night. They dated for about six months, spending time at each other's places every week. Sometimes he would leave her house in Memphis and drive for three hours to get to school before 7:30 a.m. On several occasions he went to bed in Indianola, but she would call and tell him how much she missed him, and he would pack up his things and get on the road to her, talking to her all the way. After about three hours, she would tell him to hold on a moment because someone was ringing her doorbell. She would be very shocked and ecstatic to find him standing there at the door.

She replicated the gesture many times in the course of the intense relationship. However, the romance suddenly ended in December 2005, when Austin traveled to Cameroon to defend his PhD thesis. He was gone for three weeks, during which she hardly answered his phone calls or responded to his text messages, not to mention return his calls. He was baffled by her behavior.

On January 3, 2006, he called and left a voice message stating that his defense had gone exceptionally well. Twenty minutes later, he received a text message from her essentially stating that she was seeing her ex-boyfriend, because she could not cope with being away from her man for more than forty-eight hours. He had been gone for more than two weeks. He shook his head, smiled, and decided to move on. There were too many other fish in the sea to be distraught over the loss of one.

When he returned to Indianola, his terminal degree gave him a significant pay raise and boosted respect for him in the school district and in the community. Even though the latter was immediate, the former took a few months because he had to get his credentials evaluated and, after that, apply for a doctoral-level Mississippi teacher's license, the quadruple-A license.

He was not satisfied with the evaluation done by one credential-evaluation company in New York, a member of the National Association of Credential Evaluators (NACE). So he asked them to redo the job. Three months later, they did an even more terrible evaluation. So he sent his documents to another NACE member company in Florida. The evaluation done by the other evaluator was different from the first two but did not show that the evaluators had the slightest idea of the educational system in Cameroon. For instance, his bachelor's degree was given the equivalent of almost an American high-school diploma and his master's degree the equivalent of a bachelor's degree. They also indicated that he had taken some postgraduate courses that did not culminate in a degree.

That got him wondering how NACE could claim to have uniform standards for all its member credential evaluators, yet the three evaluations of the same credentials he had received were completely different from one another. He decided to send his transcripts to three other NACE member credential evaluators and appealed the last evaluation he had received from the evaluator in Florida. The results he got, almost four months later, were mind blowing.

As he had suspected, all four new evaluations were completely different from one another and had nothing similar to the previous three. "Seven evaluations of the exact same transcripts and seven entirely different results," he murmured. He concluded that the credential-evaluation business was a fraud and entirely ridiculous. He did some research online and found that millions of other foreign-educated individuals in the United States did not disagree with his assessment of the credential-evaluation industry. There were all kinds of horror stories from people who had dealt with those companies in the past.

Not only were the evaluations incredibly expensive and never ready when needed, but those companies ensured that their clients would be stuck with them forever. For instance, a completed evaluation was good for only two years. After two years, one could not get copies of one's previously completed evaluation because, according to the credential evaluators, the educational systems of foreign nations changed so often.

Therefore, every two years, one needed a completely different evaluation, and that meant paying the new evaluation fees and waiting for several months before getting results, which might not even be satisfactory. The fact was, even if the educational system of a country changed, it would not retroactively invalidate the degrees and diplomas of previous graduates. That would mean that every degree or diploma holder would have to go back to school to fulfill whatever requirements were added to the degree or diploma program. If the University of Memphis had to add a new course or reformulate or revamp some of the courses in the bachelor's degree in their linguistics program, would that affect everybody who has ever graduated from that university with a degree in linguistics? Would those who graduated years before the change was made have less or more of a degree than students currently enrolled in the program? Would they have to come and get new transcripts reflecting the change?

One of the evaluations did recognize his doctoral degree, although it also equated one of his two master's degrees to a bachelor's degree in the United States. He chose not to appeal that one, not because he had already spent a fortune trying to confirm the shady practices in the credential-evaluation business. He was sick and tired of the ridiculousness of the credential-evaluation system.

He sent the evaluation results to the Mississippi Department of Education in Jackson, and within a few days, he received his four-A license, which he took to the school board to get his pay raise. To his surprise, the raise was retroactive, effective January 3, the day he defended his thesis.

Chapter Twenty-Four

In Too Deep

While Austin was actively pursuing his credential evaluation and pay increase, his social life was entangling. A lady he had been seeing for about six months informed him that she was pregnant. At first he thought that was impossible because he had always used protection with her, but it eventually dawned on him that one afternoon a month prior, he had had sex with her without a condom. Even then, he had taken the precaution of ejaculating outside her vagina. "I guess the precum sealed the deal," he thought.

He wasn't ready to be a father, but he wasn't going to force another girlfriend to have an abortion either. He had already done it more than thrice with three other ladies. After extensive pondering, he decided to inform his parents. They told him that he should be a man and do the right thing—get married to her and be a good father to his child. He agreed with them about the latter, but he had serious concerns about the former.

The lady already had two children, who were seven and nine, and the thought of becoming a father of three in an instant traumatized him. Additionally, Kimberly, the lady in question, had told him a few weeks earlier that she had cheated on him with one of her colleagues, a white guy, but she had insisted that they had not had sex. They had done everything else but that. She had blamed the incident on Austin's absence and lack of attention. He was angry, but after a few hours, he got over it because he had been doing the same thing with multiple other women, some who were people she knew.

The following Sunday he went to church to pray for God's guidance. He knew he had strayed from the Lord by living a life of carelessness and frivolousness, and the new pregnancy seemed like another warning from heaven for him to get his act together. He took the silent word of caution seriously, and, after mass, he went to the mall in Greenville and purchased an engagement ring, which he gave to Kimberly the next day in a very untraditional and unconventional manner.

He took her out to dinner after work, and on their way back, he reached into the glove compartment, took out the ring, gave it to her, and asked her to marry him, all while driving. Without hesitating, she agreed to be his wife. From then on things took a dizzying pace.

Chapter Twenty-Five

Dysfunctional Marriage

Irrespective of their enormous and irreconcilable differences, Austin and Kimberly got married on Friday, May 13, 2007. He was an ultraliberal who believed in God, but he also strongly believed in human imperfection and in the freedom of people to do whatever they wanted to do as long as they did not encroach upon the freedoms of others. He strongly despised individuals who judged or discriminated against others on the basis of their religion, race, gender, sexuality, ethnicity, looks, marital status, socioeconomic background, language and/or accent, and so on. Additionally, he was highly allergic to violence, ignorance, and hypocrisy.

Conversely, his spouse was a Bible-wielding, ultraconservative, Pentecostal Christian who permanently wore her religion on her sleeve. Even though she already had two children and had openly admitted to dating a long list of men and doing some sexually deviant things in the past, she persistently told Austin that she did not believe in premarital sex. The rare occasions that they slept together were only the result of his aggressive charm offensive, aided by overt threats to seek satisfaction elsewhere.

Similarly, she did not believe in drinking alcohol because it was "the devil's drink," but she often drank wine when she would come over when they were dating. She also drank Corona whenever they hung out with friends. Even though she knew that he drank wine at every meal, she banned all forms of alcohol in the house once they got married, insisting that she did not want the devil in her house.

She also banned certain types of music, including all African music, blues, and rap from the house, even though she had had no issues with them when they were dating and he played them all the time, especially music from his home country, Cameroon. She called those types of music the devil's music.

Gospel music, biblical verses, and sermons by Pentecostal preachers played on the CD player all day and all night in the living room and in the kids' bedrooms. Additionally, she had admired the fact that he was a practicing Catholic and went to church on Sundays while they were dating, but after the wedding, the Catholic Church immediately became a fake and unserious church that was engaged in idol worship and other ungodly practices. In short, it was the devil's church. The only good church was her family's.

In spite of all those differences, which caused arguments constantly, Austin persevered and stayed in the marriage for the sake of their unborn baby. His resolve became stronger after their daughter was born at the end of that year. She was 100 percent black, phenomenally beautiful, and looked just like him. He heaved a sigh of relief when he cut the umbilical cord and the doctor handed her to him, because, even though her mother had sworn that she did not have sex with her white colleague, Austin was not totally certain. And that had occurred around the time she had gotten pregnant.

In the midst of all the turmoil going on at home, Austin decided to focus his attention on his daughter. She became a significant source of comfort and solace. She inspired him to seek a bigger and better place to stay.

Austin and his wife sought financing to buy a house, but their application was declined due to her bad credit. However, the loan officer at Community Bank in Indianola said that he would approve it if her name was taken off the application, because Austin had excellent credit. With the loan approved, he picked a lot, a house plan, and all the accessories, and a brand-new home was built for his family in the classiest residential area in Indianola. The house was picture perfect, and it added to his pride and joy. He loved coming home to its beauty, spaciousness, and huge yard.

Unfortunately, the joy brought by the house soon morphed into financial stress. His wife was not helping him with the mortgage, nor was she assisting with any of the utility bills, even though she and the children would sleep with the lights and the television on all night. In fact, those energy consumers were on for more than seventeen hours on weekdays and for twenty-four hours on weekends.

He complained, screamed, yelled, and threatened to have the lights cut off, but it didn't change anything. The arguments became fiercer and more frequent, and by June 2008, he began to weigh the possibility of a divorce. The thought of leaving his daughter scared him into looking at another option, marital counseling. But when he suggested it to Kimberly, her response was "The only person who can counsel me is my mother or my father." He was not going for that. He told her that they needed to see a professional marriage counselor, someone they did not know, someone who would be fair and objective. "My parents or no counseling" was her response. The cancer kept spreading.

Early on July 4, 2008, around 4:00 a.m., Austin received a phone call from his older sister in Yaoundé, Cameroon, announcing the passing of his father. His misfortunes were just stacking up, and the stack was getting too high, blocking his view ahead of him. But his faith and hope remained stellar. He traveled to Cameroon for his father's funeral and spent two weeks there.

He was happy to see his family after almost three years, although the reunion did not occur in the best circumstances. When family and friends asked him about his wife and daughter and married life, he gave them responses that were miles away from the truth. He didn't want them to be worried about him. Also, he was ashamed of what his life had become, completely due to his own recklessness. The time away from the home drama in Indianola allowed him to reflect, recalibrate, and refocus.

Unfortunately, more devastating news was waiting for him as soon as he returned home to Indianola. While he was gone, utility bills and the mortgage bill had come in the mail, and a few were past due. Even though she had three children at home, including an eight-month-old baby, his wife did not think that it would be a great idea to assist with the light bill, even just that one time that her husband was out of the country for her father-in-law's funeral. As much as she and the kids used electricity to run appliances and keep the lights on all day and night, one would think taking care of the $320 light bill would be a matter of urgency to her at that point.

But it was not. A much bigger priority for her was to unenroll the two older children from public school and enroll them in a private school without informing her husband. She also paid the $2,000 deposit at the new school. What if the utilities were disconnected? She probably would have taken the kids to her parents' and stayed there until Austin returned and paid the bills to restore them.

He was livid when he found out what had happened, but like the provider that he had become, he found the means to take care of the bills. He decided at that point that it was no longer plausible holding on to a marriage that was sinking him deeper and deeper into financial quicksand.

Consequently, he met with an attorney to seek legal counsel. The lawyer asked him multiple questions, including whether he and his spouse had sought marital counseling. He told him the response that she had given him when he had suggested going to see a marriage counselor, and the lawyer was baffled. Then he asked about the children, especially Austin's little less-than-one-year-old princess. Tears swelled up in Austin's eyes. He could not just abandon her like that, he thought. The attorney read his mind and said, "Go home and think about it. Just let me know what you want to do, and we'll go from there."

When he returned home that evening, he again brought up the issue of counseling and got the exact same response as the first time. Then she added, "If it is not my mom and my dad, then the only other person who could counsel me is Pastor Williams." Pastor Williams was a very close friend of her parents. They even swapped pulpits on Sundays regularly. Additionally, he was the owner of the private school where she had just enrolled the older children without consulting with him. Austin did not like the idea, and he announced to her that he would be pursuing a divorce if things did not change drastically.

The next day, they talked about some changes that needed to be made, among which was her financial participation in the upkeep of the household. The issue of the father of the older children contributing in taking care of them was also raised. She said she did not know where he was and did not have the money to take him to court. Austin didn't believe that. He had not believed it the first one hundred times that he had heard it in the past. So he said that he would pay half of the legal costs to pursue the guy for child support. It was an offer she could not refuse. She very hesitantly accepted.

Within a few weeks, the fellow had been located in a neighboring town and taken to court. The judge ordered him to pay $250 monthly for the two children because he said that he did not have a job. Although Austin never saw a dime of the money the first time it was due, she told him that she had received it. The next month she broke the news to him that the payment had not been received, and the guy was nowhere to be found.

By that time the marriage was hanging by a very thin thread due to financial problems, lack of support from Kimberly, and the absolute disrespect of Austin by the older children, who told him that their grandmother had said that he could not discipline them. In fact, once when he told his stepson to turn the lights in his room off since it was noon and bright outside, the child ignored him, and when he told him if he did not turn it off, he would take away the video games that he was playing, the child said, "You can't do that! My grandma said that you can't discipline me. Only my mama can discipline me." At that point, Austin called his wife to the room and asked the young man to repeat what he had just said. He did, and she did not say or do anything, even after being told how they had gotten to that point in the first place. The encounter galvanized Austin's resolve to bring the endless nightmare to an end.

He had to do something urgently to address the situation. He felt as if he were losing his mind. He had been thinking about getting a degree in school leadership in order to boost his career and earning potential. When he spoke to the graduate-programs coordinator at the college of education at Delta State University in Cleveland, Mississippi, he learned that with his PhD, he could take a year to get a specialist degree in school leadership. The lady added that the specialist was essentially all the course work needed before one could write a dissertation to get a doctorate. That sounded to Austin like getting into a doctoral program and quitting halfway, and he was not a quitter. "How long does it take to complete the dissertation after the specialist?" he asked.

"A year, if you work hard," the coordinator said.

"Well, then that's what I would like to do. When I finish the course work to get the specialist, I want to just continue into the dissertation to get the doctorate in school leadership."

He started school that spring. It was almost therapeutic to him, as it took his mind away from the hell he was living at home.

He also sought part-time jobs to supplement his income. He got a job with Mississippi Virtual School to teach English and took and passed the certification test to become a rater for the Language Arts PRAXIS program at Educational Testing Service. Although those two opportunities did add a few hundred dollars extra to his income, they were not consistent. The virtual school lasted about five months a year, while the PRAXIS was only scored a few days a week, about five times a year. Thus, those sources of extra cash were not enough to stem the tide. He was bleeding profusely and needed something bigger and better. One thing he did have was the resolve to keep looking and to do whatever it would take to get out of that endlessly long, dark tunnel.

Chapter Twenty-Six

Lightbulb Moment

In August 2009, he was invited to the ETS campus in Princeton, New Jersey, to serve on a panel that would set new standards for the foreign-language PRAXIS test. When he landed at the Newark international airport, he found a lady, probably in her early fifties, holding a huge sign with his name on it. He walked up to her and introduced himself. She was visibly shocked.

"When they told me to come pick up Dr. Austin Annenkeng, I thought I would be picking up an older gentleman," she said. Austin smiled warmly and followed her to the waiting-stretch limousine. She put his luggage in the trunk and opened the rear right passenger door for him.

On the way to his hotel, she praised him for being so young yet smart to the point where international companies were seeking his expertise to improve the quality of their products. He thanked her for the compliments, and then she asked, "Are you married?"

After a hesitation that seemed to last about a minute, he said, "Yes."

"Why did you take so long to respond?"

"Because sometimes I wonder if I'm really married."

"Why?"

"Endless disrespect, drama, hypocrisy, and lack of financial support from my wife."

"If it's that bad, then why are you still in the marriage?"

"To be honest with you, the only thing keeping me in it now is my daughter. She's my pride and joy, and I just can't see myself being without her."

"That's the mistake many people make. They stay in a toxic marriage because of their children, but they don't realize that the toxicity of the marriage is corroding the children as well, thus scarring them emotionally and psychologically for life."

She said that she had stayed with a chronically abusive husband for twenty-five years because she did not want to leave her children and did not want them to grow up without their father in their life. But those children saw her husband and her fight and quarrel daily. Sometimes they would lock themselves up in their rooms and weep for hours. It was only after speaking to a counselor after twenty-five years, when the abuse had taken a severe physical and mental toll on her and her children, that she realized the mistake that she had been making for two and a half decades: staying in a decaying marriage. She filed for divorce the very next day and vowed to spend the rest of her life making things right by her children.

That conversation was a wake-up call to Austin. He thought about how his horrible marriage could be affecting his daughter. Though she was not old enough to realize or understand what was happening around her, between her father and her mother, the toxic situation at home was robbing her of the paternal relationship and attention that she deserved.

That was because Austin had started spending very little time at home. He would come home at night when she was sleeping and leave for work in the morning when she was sleeping or barely awake. All she was getting from him for several months were the good-night and good-bye kisses. But he was too distracted by the chaos to even realize the damage he was doing to his little princess.

That limousine ride changed his life. That limousine driver reframed his perspective on things. Right there, in the back seat, he vowed to get out of that corrosive marriage before it was too late. He thanked the driver, Mellisa, for helping him understand the risk and peril involved in staying in a bad relationship for the sake of children.

After five days of intense deliberations with other foreign-language experts from around the United States, Austin's panel adopted new standards for the foreign-language PRAXIS assessment. There were times during the five days when thoughts of what he had to do upon his return home distracted him, and he struggled to refocus his attention to the work he had been flown out to Princeton to do. Nevertheless, his contribution to the panel discussions was remarkable, and ETS showed him their gratitude.

He arrived home a day early, on Saturday evening instead of Sunday, when he was expected. There was an unfamiliar car in the middle of the driveway, blocking the entrance to the garage. He parked right behind it and got out in the light rain that had started falling. As he approached the front door, several voices could be heard coming from inside the house. He opened the door with his key and went in. Sitting in his living room, in his favorite seat, was the father of his stepchildren, the guy he had been told had disappeared without a trace and had stopped paying child support. He had brought six of his other children to see the two who lived with Austin.

"Hello, Dr. Annenkeng!" he said.

"Good evening, Cedric. How have you been?"

"I've been great."

"You've been missing. The last time we heard from you was ages ago."

At that moment, something caught Austin's eye in the huge mirror above the seat where Cedric was sitting. It was Kimberly, who was standing in the kitchen on the opposite side of the living room. She made a gesture with her hand across her neck. Back in Cameroon, that gesture would have meant killing someone, but his students had told him during a discussion of cultural differences that in United States, it meant stop. Kimberly was giving Cedric a sign to not respond to the question that Austin had asked. He either ignored the sign, or he did not see it.

"That's not true. I see my children very often. I also call your house phone regularly to speak to them."

Austin was shocked. He could not believe what he had just heard. "Does that mean you've been paying child support too?"

"Of course! I've never missed a payment."

Austin was livid, but he didn't show it. He stayed calm and courteous, even after the guests had left.

The following Monday he met with an attorney in Greenville to seek legal counsel regarding a divorce. He recounted the story of his marriage, from the inception up to his decision to leave. The lawyer said that he had handled thousands of cases like Austin's over his forty-three-year career, some worse than what he was describing. After asking a series of questions and listening intently to Austin's responses, during which he copiously took notes, he told him that if everything was true, he had a very good case, but that it would be even better if his wife were the one to file for the divorce. The lawyer explained that the judges tended to favor the women, especially when there were children involved. He said that in order to not appear as if he were abandoning his wife and children, it would be wiser to let her file for the divorce. And from the way things were going as described by Austin, it wouldn't be long before she would do exactly that.

"However, if you insist, we can start the process today. But as an attorney—an excellent one, for that matter—I have to tell you the best course of action."

Austin agreed to wait and returned home. He continued taking care of things at home as he had always done, even though he was very upset by recent discoveries. He also started spending more time at home with his daughter. One Saturday morning in mid-September 2009, Kimberly, who had been acting warmly and kindly toward him since he had found her ex-boyfriend in his house, revived the issue of marital counseling. She was ready to see a professional marriage counselor anywhere, to fix their marriage, but Austin was no longer interested. He didn't think that she was being honest about anything, especially about saving her marriage. She was probably just troubled by the fact that he did not express anger over finding her ex in his house or over the secret that the ex had revealed regarding seeing and talking to his children regularly and being current on his child-support payments. That must have been bothering her tremendously.

She continued to act kindly after failing to get him to see a marriage counselor. On his birthday on October 16, she bought him a guitar and took him out to dinner at the Garfield's in Greenville. When they returned home that night, the pampering continued, and before he could come to his senses, they were both naked in bed and having sex, something he had been deprived of for a very long time.

A month later, she missed her period and announced to him that she was pregnant. He was not excited about the news. Back when their daughter was born, he had told her that he did not want any more children, and she had agreed. From time to time after then, she would express the desire for one more child, but he would remind her that they could not afford it, that he could not afford it, since he was the only one taking care of the bills. On the extremely rare occasions that they had sex, he made sure to wear a condom—except on that fateful night of extreme passion on his last birthday.

Without his asking, she announced with gusto that she was going to keep the baby. She also added that she was going to get a divorce and that the judge would let her keep the house and the cars and make him pay for it in addition to paying her alimony; child support; and medical, vision, dental, and life insurance for the children. When he told her that she could not get a house that she had not spent a dime for the purchase and upkeep of, her response was "No judge would put a pregnant woman out of the marital home." It would be an understatement to say that Austin was terrified.

Chapter Twenty-Seven

The Tipping Point

The next morning he called the attorney that he had spoken to a few weeks earlier, but he was not available. He called again five times that day to no avail, so after school he drove to Greenville to see if he could meet with him for even a minute. He just wanted to know if Kimberly was telling the truth that she would take away everything that he had worked so hard for. When he got to the lawyer's office, he was met with some more bad news. The attorney had died two days earlier. Austin was distraught, and he went into panic mode for several weeks. That ruined Christmas, even though he tried to act normally when he was at home, especially around his daughter.

He was slightly relieved when school resumed after the Christmas break. Work gave him something else to think of other than losing everything to an undeserving spouse. That relief did not last for long, as at 9:45 a.m. on February 10, 2010, a sheriff deputy knocked on his classroom door and asked him to step outside. His principal, who had accompanied the deputy, watched his class while he was out. The deputy served him divorce papers and left.

Noticing that Austin was visibly distraught and understanding that he was in no shape to effectively teach for the rest of the day, the principal, who liked and respected Austin greatly and had been through a divorce a couple of times himself, advised him to go find a lawyer. He sent the librarian to take care of his class for the remainder of the day. The principal also recommended a very good divorce attorney in Cleveland. Austin called the attorney, and he told him to come that same day, with the papers that he had been served.

The office of Lewis & Trump was a fifteen-minute drive from his school. He sat in the waiting room for eight minutes, and then a white man in his late fifties came out of one of the offices down the hallway and walked toward him with his right hand extended.

"Good morning! I am Donald Lewis. I understand you need some legal advice."

"Good morning! I am Austin Annenkeng. I would like some help with a divorce. I got served at work less than an hour ago."

"Well, you've come to the right place. Follow me to my office so I can look at what you have."

They both sat on a couch in the attorney's office while he carefully read the divorce papers. After every paragraph the lawyer blurted out a loud "Wow" and shook his head. That frightened Austin, who had been too shaken to even read what the deputy had served him. Then, after about fifteen minutes of reading, Mr. Lewis said, "She wants to take everything away from you—cars, house, retirement, children, child support, alimony, and so on. She also wants you to pay for the house's upkeep."

"She told me a few weeks ago that she was going to do that."

"She cites irreconcilable differences as the reason for the divorce. She also claims that you cheated on her."

"I did not cheat on her."

Austin went on to describe with specific details the hell he had been living in from the beginning of the marriage up to the moment he got served.

"If you've only been married for three years, then she is not entitled to alimony, according to Mississippi law," the lawyer said. Austin was happy to hear that. "She's right that the judges are usually sympathetic toward pregnant women, but if you have proof that she contributed to neither the purchase of the house nor its upkeep and running in the course of the marriage, I could fight for you to keep it. Are all the papers in your name?"

"Yes."

"I'm not going to promise you a favorable outcome, but if you would like, I would file a countersuit."

"That's exactly what I want. I'm not going to let her just take away everything that I've worked hard for."

They agreed on a fee, and Austin wrote a check for the $1,500 retainer. A refund anticipation loan for $1,450 had hit his account earlier that morning. Perfect timing!

"I need you to bring me all the documentation that we've discussed and anything else that you think might be helpful in this case. I also want you to remain calm during this process. It could be long and messy, but regardless of how messy things get, do not rock the boat."

Austin shook Mr. Lewis's hand in agreement and left.

When he returned home later that day, there was a brand-new Nissan Pathfinder in the garage, in the spot where Kimberly always parked her Nissan Sentra. He wondered whom it belonged to and what the person might be doing in his house, but when he got into the house, there was no stranger. Kimberly was in the kitchen cooking while the kids were watching TV in the living room. He also noticed the new car keys on a Tom Wadler Nissan folder right next to Trisha's purse on the kitchen countertop.

"So in anticipation of all the things she's asking in the divorce suit, she's traded her old car for a bigger and better one," he said under his breath.

He greeted Kimberly warmly, as if nothing had happened, and proceeded to play with the kids for a few minutes before going to his room. He noticed in his closet that someone had been through his personal things. His briefcase, where he kept his important papers, was open, and there were documents hanging out of it, as if someone had searched the briefcase in a hurry. He checked to ensure that nothing was missing and resolved not to say anything about it or about the divorce papers he had been served at work.

The divorce process snailed its way through the court while Austin stayed calm. He didn't say a word about it to his soon-to-be ex-wife even though they lived under the same roof and had shared the same bed up to mid-May 2010. She was secretly hoping that he would leave the house, thus making it easier for her to get it, while he was determined to put up a ferocious fight for what he had worked extremely hard for. By the end of April, the attorney's fees were getting so high that he started using the mortgage money to pay the lawyer. Things were getting extremely difficult financially. Apart from not being able to pay all the household bills, he struggled to find food to eat, even though Kimberly cooked very good meals every day. After she and her children ate their fill, she emptied the leftovers into the garbage. Austin still didn't say anything.

Then on May 15, 2010, he returned home from work to find the Nissan Pathfinder parked in the middle of the garage, preventing him access to his parking spot. He got out of his car in the heavy rain and opened the door leading into the kitchen through the garage. He found Trisha watching TV in the living room. The children were not home.

"Could you please move your car to your parking spot so I could park mine?" he requested. She ignored him. He repeated the request again and again and again, calmly. She did not budge. He dropped the subject and went to the kitchen to check if some pinto beans that he had bought in December were still good to cook. He found the bag of beans in one of the cabinets near the stove. They didn't look spoiled. He poured them into a pot and opened the faucet at the sink to clean the beans. At that moment and without warning, Kimberly appeared at his right, sandwiching him between her and the refrigerator, on his left. She was seven months pregnant and had gained a considerable amount of weight, more than 50 pounds above her usual 160 pounds.

With as much force as she could apply with all her weight, she bumped him with her left side, particularly her left hip, sending him flying into the refrigerator and spilling the pot of pinto beans all over the kitchen. He hit his head against the refrigerator. She was clearly looking for trouble. After waiting in vain for more than two months for him to react angrily or say something about the divorce that she had filed, she had decided to step her game up to the level of physical provocation and assault. He did not take the bait. He stepped out of the kitchen into the garage and called the police and his lawyer, but the latter had already closed for the day, as it was already 5:20 p.m.

The cops arrived within three minutes. He told them what had happened, from the car parked in the middle of the garage up to the provocation in the kitchen. They told him that she had the right to park her car anywhere on the property since they were still legally married. However, they went into the house to talk, to persuade her to move her car to the side and let him park his car. As for the assault, he chose not to press the matter further. While the police officers were in the house talking to her, he stood outside, leaning on his car.

At that moment, Kimberly's mother sped into the yard and parked her car on the lawn. As soon as she jumped out of the car, she started shouting, "What did you call the police over here for? What did you call the police over here for? What's gonna happen to you, not even the police will be able to stop it." The threat was loud enough for everyone in the house and the neighbors to hear. She then ran toward the kitchen door, but it opened as the police officers and Trisha were coming out. The former greeted her warmly and respectfully. She was their boss's older sister.

Austin could not believe what was happening to him—the deprivation of his parking spot, the provocation, the threat, and the police pleading with Kimberly to move her car. He had expected them to act deliberately and forcefully. He had not done anything wrong. He had acted calmly in a situation that clearly could have spun tragically out of control, but there they were almost coddling her, as if she were the victim. Was it because she was their boss's niece, or was it that the law was always on the woman's side, as some had tried to make him believe? He was scared. He didn't know what to do. He couldn't think clearly. Something told him to get his key and get the hell out of there. He did, with the police, Trisha, and her mother still in the driveway.

As he was driving on the 448 heading toward Cleveland, he called a friend and doctoral classmate, Chad, and told him what he had just come out of. The friend invited him for a beer. Austin and Chad sat in his garage all night and drank Bud Light and talked about doctoral assignments that were due, about the school year that was inching to a close, and about books they would coauthor after graduating. They both avoided the elephant in the room until Austin said it was time for him to return home. At that moment, Chad went into the house and then returned with a huge, dusty duffel bag, which he placed gently between their seats.

"I'm not letting you leave here today without getting good shit to protect yourself, bruh," Chad said, and he unzipped the bag to reveal an astounding stash of guns, enough for an entire army unit in Cameroon. The closest Austin had ever been to a firearm in his entire life was watching Hollywood movies and TV shows. He didn't like them. Finding a bullet in an apartment he had just moved into five years earlier had unsettled him to the point where he had dialed 911 to report it and get help disposing of it. There were all kinds of guns in the bag—long, short, automatic, and semiautomatic.

"Take your pick," Chad said.

"I don't need that shit, man, and besides, I don't like guns."

Chad insisted unsuccessfully and conceded with "I'm here for you, bruh. I got your back. Call me if that bitch and her crazy folks dare to do something to you."

He gave Austin a protracted shoulder bump and told him to be very careful.

Austin got home that night around eleven thirty. Everybody in his household had already gone to bed. Kimberly was in her oldest child's bed, where she had been sleeping for some weeks. Only the voice of a popular Pentecostal minister preaching about combating the devil and evil spirits could be heard coming from the radio in that room. Austin noticed cross marks on the walls in the corridors and in the living room. There was a much larger cross drawn on the door of the master bedroom, where he slept. Kimberly had started drawing these signs using blessed olive oil after filing for divorce. The oil was ruining the paint on the walls and doors, but his repeated complaints only led to him being called "demon," "evil," "devil," and every other name for evil in the Bible.

He went into his bedroom and pulled the bed to block the door just in case Kimberly or her numerous allies were to attempt to do something to him. They had scared him enough earlier to render him paranoid, but he was not going to resort to carrying a gun for protection. He was going to do simple, nonviolent, and proactive things to stay safe until the end of the storm.

The next morning everyone except his daughter gave him a frosty, steely look as he was preparing to leave for work. He was unbothered by that. When he got to work, the superintendent and the principal came to his classroom during his planning period at 9:30 a.m. to check on him. The former had been his principal and host father when he arrived in the Mississippi Delta six years earlier. He too had recently been through a very messy divorce after twenty-five years of marriage. Austin recounted to them the events of the previous twenty-four hours, and they advised him to remain calm. The superintendent, Mr. Brown, said, "This too shall pass. I promise you, son!"

He called his lawyer, Donald Lewis, whom he just called Don, when his bosses left. He narrated to him what had happened the previous day, and the seasoned attorney was pleased with the way his client had handled the situation. However, the man of law warned him one more time that his wife would continue to try different tricks to make him lose his mind and react foolishly, but that he should continue to exercise restraint and avoid her as much as possible. Don also hinted that the attorney for the other side was getting frustrated with his client, who, in his words, "was acting like she woke up on a different planet every day."

"Austin, they're getting desperate. I need you to stay calm and to not rock the boat while I work to get this matter over with," Don said.

On his way home from work, he stopped at KFC to get something to eat for dinner. While there, a lady approached him and expressed her deepest sympathy for what he was traversing. She said, "Her mother gave her the money and encouraged her to file for the divorce. She told her to take everything from you. They would like to move their church into your much bigger living room." He thanked her and continued eating. He was not surprised by what she had revealed to him. That wanted his house at all costs.

A week later Austin was getting ready to leave work when Don called frantically. "Austin, where are you?"

"I'm still at work. I'll be going home in a few minutes."

"No! Don't go home," the lawyer said. "Your wife, her parents, and some friends are over there as we speak. They're moving her belongings out of the house. They're giving up on the house. I don't want you to go over there and they do something to you out of anger."

"That's very good news. Thank you! Thank you, Don!"

"Her lawyer called me moments ago to inform me. He's ready for this case to be over. So you just hang in there. The end is near."

"Thank you very much. I have a class at Delta State tonight. I'll just go there from here."

"That's a good idea. I'll call you when I have something new."

Austin could barely pay attention in class that night. He was very eager to go home to see what the movers had taken. When he finally got to the house, all the furniture in the living room, dining room, breakfast area, and bedrooms were gone. The picture frames, paintings, and other decorations had been yanked off the walls, causing severe damage. The chandeliers in the living room, dining room, and foyer had been ripped from the ceiling. The kitchen was also empty. There was trash and debris everywhere from the damaged walls and broken objects. The only items left behind were a couch and a bed from his bachelor pad, two TV sets, his guitars, and his clothes. Nevertheless, he was very happy that his house was going to remain in his hands, however damaged and empty. He vowed to repair and replace everything as soon as he had the means. The next day he bought new locks for the entrances.

On May 27, he received a text message from Kimberly stating that something was wrong with the pregnancy and that she was being rushed to the hospital by her mother. He responded that he was on his way. When he got there, she had already been placed in a room, and the doctors had started making preparations to deliver the baby, more than two months before he was due to arrive. Her blood pressure was through the roof, and she was having extremely painful contractions. The atmosphere in the room was tense, to say the least, especially when the doctors and nurses left and it was just Austin, Kimberly, and her mother left. They didn't say a word to him and also ignored all the questions he asked about her plight and what would happen to the baby if he came early. At 4:30 p.m., after ignoring him for over three hours, the women ordered him to leave. They said that they would call him with any updates. He had not heard from them when he went to bed around 10:40 p.m.

He called as soon as he woke up the following morning, but neither Kimberly nor her mother answered the phone. He texted and called again multiple times in the course of the day but to no avail. Finally, on May 29, he found out from one of Kimberly's cousins that the baby had been taken out prematurely on May 28 and had been placed in an incubator. They had not called him or texted him with updates, as they had said. He sent a text to inform her he had heard about the baby and that he was on his way to the hospital to see him. She responded instantly, saying, "Don't come over here!" He then called his lawyer to inform him and to ask for advice.

"They can't prevent you from seeing your son. I'll call her lawyer and arrange for you to see your baby and get back to you," the attorney said. A few hours went by, and then Don called with news that Austin could go see his son at 9:00 a.m. the next day.

He got to the hospital on time and was told that Kimberly had gone back home. The nurses took him to the nursery, where there were four newborn babies in cribs and a very tiny one, about the size of a can of soda, in a transparent glass case. He had multiple tubes and wires going into, out of, and on his miniscule body in many places, especially in his mouth and nostrils and on his chest. His only clothing was a doll-size hat and a tiny diaper. He looked extremely frail.

"That's your baby," the nurse said, as she pointed at the incubator.

The sight of the tiny, motionless, helpless, and innocent baby in the box provoked an earthquake of emotions in Austin, and a torrent of tears streamed from his eyes, inundating his face and shirt. He was not allowed to touch or hold the baby. All he could do was stand there and look through the glass for hours, until the visitation was over.

He returned every day at the same time for the next month. School being out for the summer allowed him to spend three hours daily watching the being in the cage morph gradually into a normal baby. After the first week, he was allowed to touch him with gloved hands through holes in the incubator. The wires and tubes everywhere on the baby made it difficult for him to rub and caress his fragile head, forehead, chest, and stomach. The baby, who had started moving very gently and seemingly painfully since his father had walked into the room, as if he had felt his presence, slightly raised his tiny right hand, and Austin reached for it. He held his boy's hand and rubbed it tenderly for a long time, and then the baby opened his closed fist to reveal his pink, fragile, and cotton-soft palm. When his father started to gently rub the palm with his index finger, the baby closed his hand again and held on to the finger for close to two hours and seventeen minutes. His father stood there, reflecting and murmuring loving and soothing words to him and sometimes calling him by the name that his mother and maternal grandmother had given him without his dad's consent.

Austin had implored Kimberly several times in the course of the pregnancy to name the baby Austin Annenkeng Jr., and she had agreed. But she colluded with her mother to name him Jacob. They had kept Austin completely in the dark regarding Jacob's birth, naming, and birth certificate. Because they had barred him from the hospital, he had not been allowed to sign the birth record of his only son. He was mentioned on the document as the father to ensure complications would not arise in their pursuit of child support. That was the only consideration they gave to him at the time Jacob was born.

A million and one things were going through his mind as he stood by Jacob's incubator with his right index finger held tightly in the baby's right fist. He thought about the evil behavior of people who claimed to be staunchly religious and even called themselves preachers. He reflected on Jacob and Jasmine growing up without him under the same roof. He pondered the overt and covert threats to his life. The cash he was bleeding as a result of the divorce also crossed his mind. The thought that his late father had never had the opportunity to meet his grandbabies crept up. These thoughts and more took deep bites at his heart and caused huge drops of tears to flood from his swollen eyes, hitting the top of the transparent incubator and streaming down the sides. At that point, with his index finger still in Jacob's clenched hand, Austin moved his thumb up and down, rubbing the baby's little hand and solemnly promising, "It's going to be all right, Jake. We're going to be all right!" Then he added, "I love you very much, and I will always be there for you."

When he left the hospital that day, he had the burning desire to see Jasmine. He had not laid eyes on or spoken to her since her mother had moved out. An overwhelming courage drove him straight to the home of his in-laws. Kimberly's father was getting groceries out of his truck in the driveway when Austin arrived. Out of caution, he parked at the curb, came out of his car, and shouted, "Good afternoon, Mr. Elder. I was wondering if I could see my daughter, Jasmine." He could see her through the screen door jumping with excitement at the sight of her father.

The man turned around and walked toward Austin and then stopped in the middle of the driveway, with bags of groceries in both hands. Then he said frostily, "I don't want you over here. Don't you ever come here again!"

Something in his eyes terrified Austin more than the warning that was coming out of his mouth. Without responding, he rushed to his car, cranked it up, and drove off. He could hear the screams and wailing of the toddler emanating from inside the house, as if on a loudspeaker. Tears filled his eyes and blurred his vision. He pulled over to the side of the road and pulled his shirt over his face to wipe the tears that were streaming down his cheeks uncontrollably. In the midst of the weeping, he looked up to heaven and said a prayer asking for God's guidance and protection.

The threat from Kimberly's father was the last straw that got Austin so frightened that as soon as he arrived home, he decided to start looking for jobs outside Indianola. The environment in Indianola had gotten dangerously unsafe for him. Kimberly and her parents either were related to or were very close to almost everybody in the small city. That made Austin, a foreigner from a country that was seventeen thousand miles away and who had no family in the United States, a potential target everywhere he went in Indianola. They would skin him alive at the very first opportunity. And with the police chief being the sibling of Kimberly's mother, anything that might happen to him may not be given the attention it deserved. There was already a tangible precedent to corroborate that feeling.

There were two French positions at Jackson Public Schools (JPS) in Jackson, ninety-two miles from Indianola. He applied for both. He also applied for teaching jobs in Memphis and Nashville. It was time to leave Indianola. He would rent out his house and go anywhere within driving distance. He needed to be able to come back regularly to see his children as soon as the courts set the guidelines for custody and visitation.

An e-mail came while he was still completing an application for Nashville Metropolitan Schools. It was from the principal of a middle school in Jackson. She wanted to know if he was available for an interview at 1:00 p.m. the next day. That was more than a miracle. He responded and confirmed his availability.

On June 10, 2010, Austin arrived at the central office of JPS for his interview. He was interviewed by a panel of three principals, each of whom was having a new school constructed and was in need of a French teacher. His credentials impressed them, but it was his responses to their questions that blew them away and had them engage in a tug-of-war to get him to commit to their school. He went with the lady who had invited him to the interview. It was the only option that was fair and made sense. If the other administrators were that interested in him, they should have responded to his application earlier.

After the interview, he drove around Jackson to look for a decent place to stay. He didn't like the two apartment complexes that he was shown downtown. The manager of the second complex directed him to one of their new communities, the Reserve of Byram, in Byram, Mississippi, a few minutes outside Jackson. It was gated and had all kinds of modern amenities, including a fully equipped gym, a swimming pool, a carwash area, cable, Internet, telephone, a fireplace, tanning beds, and more.

Austin was particularly attracted by the fact that the complex was gated. The yard was perfectly manicured, and the massive complex seemed very peaceful and quiet. It was the perfect spot for him. Even though the rent was high, he convinced himself that it was the price to pay for safety and comfort. And Lord knows that he badly needed the former. It was his sole reason for leaving Indianola.

He didn't sign the lease that day because he didn't have the money, but the manager, who had been staring at him incessantly since he had walked into her office and during the tour of the facility, told him that she could hold one of the three available units for him for a week. He needed to act fast.

Upon leaving the Reserve of Byram, he called one of his colleagues who was infatuated with his house. His wife and he had visited for a July 4 dinner the previous year, and she hadn't stopped showering praise on the building and the yard. With its four bedrooms, walk-in closets, large living room, spacious breakfast area, roomy and fully equipped kitchen, pantry, laundry room, two-car garage, and half-acre yard, the home was in the most upscale and peaceful neighborhood in Indianola. It offered the perfect environment to raise their three sons.

"Hello, Keyshaun! You know how you and your wife have been talking nonstop about your admiration of my house?"

"Yes! You're living in our dream home. Hopefully, one day we will be able to build one like that and move out of this dilapidated, crumbling, and pest-filled complex."

"Well! What if I told you that you could live in it now if you wanted to?"

"How is that possible?"

"I just got offered a job in Jackson, and with everything that has been happening to me in Indianola over the past few months, I would like to put my house up for rent or sale and move somewhere else for my safety. I wanted to let you know first before putting a sign in the yard."

"Oh, wow! This is the best news I've received in a very long time. Shameka and the boys will be ecstatic! We've been looking around for a better place that's not far from the kids' school and my wife's job, but we haven't found anything we like. We were starting to look in Cleveland, Greenville, and Greenwood. Buddy, are you sure this isn't some kind of prank?"

"No, man! If you want, I could get a lease agreement together for you to sign, and I'll be out of the house by July thirty-first."

Austin didn't need to put the house on the market. Within a week, Keyshaun and his wife signed the lease, which would go into effect on the last day of July 2010. The rent was the net amount of Austin's monthly mortgage payment. They paid a security deposit and the first month's rent, thereby enabling Austin to secure his apartment in Byram with a lease that would start on August 1. He couldn't believe how smoothly things were going.

One scorching and muggy afternoon in mid-July, he was watching TV on the couch in his bare living room when the doorbell rang. He wasn't expecting anyone, so he looked out the window and immediately recognized Kimberly's truck. His heart started racing. "What is she doing over here? What if it's someone else who's bold enough to come over here in broad daylight to do something to me?" He decided not to open the door.

But the bell kept ringing. The voice of a little girl preceded the last ring. She shouted desperately, "Daddy, open the door!"

He had not seen her in a month. As he was walking to the door, he thought he also heard the cry of a newborn in that steamy Mississippi heat. He had been at the hospital the previous day, and although he had been allowed to hold and feed Jake for the fifth time in a week, no one had told him that he was going to be discharged so soon.

Something had touched Kimberly's heart on the way from the hospital, and she had brought the children to see their father instead of taking them straight to the home of her parents, as they would have preferred. Austin reached for the baby and held him tightly in his arms, but Jasmine was not going to let him be the only one held. She had been deprived of paternal attention and love for two months, and she was not letting that go any further. With both of her hands around her father standing in the foyer, she jumped and began climbing him like a monkey climbing a tree. Realizing that he had to do something fast to avert an accident, Austin held Jacob in his left hand and picked up Jasmine with the free one and hurried to the couch. His anxiety had faded into great excitement. Jasmine sat quietly on his right lap and rested her head on his chest while squeezing him tightly with both arms around him, as if she was afraid that someone was going to attempt to take him away from her again. Meanwhile, in his left arm, Jacob was staring at his progenitor's face with a smile that said he would rather be nowhere else. Austin held on to his precious loves on one of the couches while their mother sat at the other end conspicuously staring at the ceiling and the walls.

"I see you repainted the house and replaced the chandeliers," she said.

"Yes. I did the painting all by myself, one room at a time, but I hired an electrician to replace the chandeliers. I have to get the house ready for the tenants who'll be moving in at the end of this month."

"Really? I heard that you got a job and are moving to Jackson. I'm happy for you!"

Austin was not expecting the last part of her response, and he knew that it was as fake as snow in the Sahara. He swiftly pivoted. "Thank you for bringing Jacob and Jasmine to see me. I really appreciate it. I hope this becomes consistent."

She consented and allowed him to enjoy the presence of his babies for four more hours, like someone who was seeing them for the last time.

When they left, Austin immediately grabbed a notepad and a pencil and captured on paper his thoughts and feeling about his children. He put them in the following poem:

Jacob and Jasmine
Though we do not live together,
You stay on my mind every day.
Though I do not see you every day,
I imagine being with you every day.
Though I do not talk to you every day,
Your voices resonate in my head every day.

You're my angels when I need protection.
You're my inspiration when I need restoration.
You're my motivation when I need orientation.
You're my consolation when I am in desperation.

I can't imagine not having both of you in my life, because
Without you life is pointless;
Without you life is meaningless.
Without you life is aimless;
Without you life is tasteless.

I like the way you make me feel.
I like the way you fill me with zeal.
I like the way you make me think.
I like the way you pull me from the brink.
I like the way you make me grow.
I like the way you make me glow.
I will always be thankful for you, my blessings.
I will always be there for you.
I will always love you!

Chapter Twenty-Eight

New Beginnings

July 31 came like a breeze. There were two moving trucks in the drive-way of the newest rental property in Indianola by 9:00 a.m. Furniture and boxes were being off-loaded from the first one, while the second was being loaded to head out. By noon Austin was ready to go. His lessee offered to drive the moving truck, since he knew his way around Jackson. A student of theirs, Gabriel, who had helped load the tuck, also got his parents' approval to travel with them. Austin trailed the moving truck in his 2008 Buick Lucerne.

Two hours later they were at the Reserve of Byram. Austin got his keys from the leasing office and the moving-in began. It didn't take them long to get everything out of the truck and into the second-floor, two-bedroom apartment that was going to be his home for the next two years. He had just a few belongings, including a suitcase containing his clothes and shoes, two beds and dressers, three TV sets, a coffee-table set, two lamps, a washer and dryer, two plates, and some cutlery. By the time they finished unpacking and assembling the furniture and appliances, the helpers were tired and starving. Austin asked them what and where they would like to eat, and they said they wanted some barbecue. The teen-ager, who had recently turned eighteen, also pleaded to be taken to the strip club after dinner. Austin told him that he couldn't afford to pay for their dinner and still take them to the strip club.

"What if we made some barbecue ribs ourselves in the oven? That would save some money that we could use to go to the strip club," Gabriel suggested with a look in his that said, "Please! Please! This is the dream of a lifetime!"

Austin thought about all the help and resourcefulness the young man had graciously offered him, and he decided to reward him by granting his lifelong desire.

After a long night of celebrating at the strip club, Austin and his guests returned to his apartment a little before dawn. The helper slept for a few hours in the guest bedroom before leaving in the moving truck, which they were to return in Indianola on the renter's behalf. For his part, Austin woke up in a very gorgeous, neat, and fresh-smelling apartment. He opened the double doors that led to the balcony to drink his freshly brewed coffee. He stood there for forty-five minutes, admiring the beauty of the complex.

After a few minutes, there came some murmuring voices from the balcony below him. He wondered what the individuals were talking about. Whatever it was, they clearly did not want anyone else to hear it. Then, suddenly, an elderly couple, probably in their seventies, left the balcony and stepped onto the lawn in front of their apartment, just to get a view of whoever had moved in above them. "Good morning, neighbor," the two nosy individuals shouted in unison, and they introduced themselves to as Bertha and Larry.

Then, without anyone asking them, they started spilling information randomly. They shouted what they used to do for a living, how long they had been living in their apartment, the reason why they had moved to the complex a year prior, how much they liked the place, who lived in the other six apartments in the building, who lived in the eight units in the building across the street, what they thought about each tenant in each apartment, how frivolous the previous occupant of Austin's apartment was, the number of times there were fights in there, and how thrilled they were when they found out that she was moving out. "We hope you're not going to be like her," the husband said.

Austin was going to express his displeasure with the statement, but the old lady didn't give him the opportunity to say a word, as she shouted, "He looks like a fine, responsible gentleman, Larry, doesn't he?"

"Yes, he sure does. What did you say you did for a living again?"

Austin was amused. He had not told them what he did for a living. They had only given him a second to say his name. He was not interested in all the unsolicited pieces of information that they were throwing at him, and he had only continued standing there in order to give the evidently judgmental couple no reason to brand him without even knowing him. He told them that he was a teacher with JPS, and then he pretended to take a phone call. The couple left him alone and went back to their balcony, and Austin went into his apartment.

A week after moving into his apartment, Austin started working at his new school, Cardozo Middle School. The campus was fifteen minutes away. The first week was dedicated to professional development sessions, classroom assignment, scheduling, announcement of teacher duties, and a host of other pre-school-year things. He was going to be teaching sixth- and seventh-grade French. He didn't have a preference for his classroom, since the entire school building was brand new with ultramodern furnishings. For the first time in his career, he received a brand-new Lenovo laptop for planning, instruction, and recording grades. He looked forward with excitement to the first day of teaching.

He was not disappointed when the students finally came. He had six classes of sixteen to twenty students who were eager to learn a foreign language. As he had anticipated, the kids had all kinds of questions about him, including his accent, his country of origin, his family, and his clothes. They also wanted to know if there were restaurants like McDonald's in Africa; whether Africans dressed like Americans; whether there were cars and houses in Africa; whether there were schools in Africa; whether the kids there learned the same subjects as American students; whether the students in Africa were more respectful of adults and their peers than in America; whether they had free lunch, books, and busing to school like them; how many grade levels there were in African schools; and so on. Austin obliged all their inquiries and curiosity. He even had pictures, maps, online resources, and other artifacts to support his responses. He was thrilled by the prospect of things that he could accomplish with such an inquisitive, eager, highly motivated, and competitive group of students.

Chapter Twenty-Nine

Divorce Settlement

On August 20, Austin's attorney called to inform him that the other camp wanted to settle. He discussed with the lawyer what he was comfortable with and what would be a deal breaker. Four days later he drove to Cleveland to sign the settlement. Out of the litany of things that he would have lost in the divorce if Kimberly had had her wish, Austin was only required to pay child support. He also agreed to provide health insurance to his children through his job. He was very pleased with the outcome of the eight-month-long process, which had been fraught with rage, tension, betrayal, anxiety, panic, hypocrisy, and evil. At times he felt as if he were living Jesus's journey to Golgotha, where he was crucified. In a last-ditch effort to get everything she wanted, she tried to claim that he had started seeing other women without the divorce being finalized. She sent private investigators to go talk to a lady, a bartender, whom Austin had met at a restaurant in Greenville three months earlier. The lady liked Austin immensely and looked forward to him stopping there for drinks to drown the sorrow caused by the divorce process. At times she would give him advice, especially as she had been through a divorce herself. She was just a friend. That strategy failed woefully because the bartender told the investigator the truth and notified Austin immediately.

He didn't care how far behind the divorce had set him, both financially and emotionally. He was just happy that it was finally over. He still owed his attorney $7,000 and had three more payments to catch up on, on his mortgage in Indianola. He probably should have paused to evaluate the impact of the divorce on his wallet and to develop effective strategies to regain control of his finances. He also needed to come up with effective ways to tackle the other roadblocks that dealing with the custodial parent of a newborn and a toddler would certainly entail. In the words of Mr. Brown, his former boss and friend, he needed to "get ready for damn foolishness and ridiculousness for eighteen years and even beyond."

It wasn't long before the first of these ridiculous situations would creep up. According to the divorce agreement, he was supposed to have his children every other weekend. The first pickup was hitch free, but two days before he was to pick them up for another weekend, he called to inform Kimberly of the time and location of the pickup. They agreed to meet at McDonald's in Indianola at 5:00 p.m. Austin would drive there immediately after leaving work. During his lunch break on that day, he sent a text message to Kimberly to confirm the appointment. "We will be there," she responded.

With much excitement and anticipation, he drove the one-and-a-half-hour distance, at times going fifteen to twenty miles per hour above the posted speed limit, in order to get there in time. The thought of a newborn baby and a three-year-old sitting in a car in a fast-food restaurant parking lot was unsettling to him. He arrived at 4:58 p.m., but they were not there. He waited for five minutes and then five more, but still no Kimberly. He picked up his phone and dialed her number.

"Hello!" she answered.

"I'm here at McDonald's," he said. And then he asked, "Are you on your way?"

"We're in Starkville."

"But you confirmed on Wednesday and four hours ago that you would meet me here today at five p.m."

"I know I said that, but we came up here with my boyfriend, and we won't be back until Sunday evening. You're welcome to wait in Indianola until then to see them."

She hung up before Austin could utter another word. He was stunned and couldn't believe what was happening. He thought about what Mr.

Brown had warned him about just a few weeks earlier and resigned himself in prayer to the Lord: "Lord, I entrust this situation into your hands. Let your will be done," he said, before getting back on the road to Byram.

The following Friday, he took off work to complete a practicum project for his doctoral program. The principal he had to complete the project with was in Greenville, just thirty minutes away from Indianola. They wrapped up earlier than he expected, a little after noon. With plenty of time to spare, he decided to surprise his children at their day-care center before returning to Byram.

The babies, especially Jasmine, were ecstatic when he appeared in their classroom. He held them, fed them, and played with them. When naptime came, they fought off sleep just to be with him. He had been there for about two hours when Kimberly rushed into the room with a thirtysomething-year-old guy and snatched both children from him and gave them to the man. She told him to take them to the car and then turned to Austin and yelled without regard or consideration, "You don't have the right to come and see them here without my permission."

"I'm their father. It's not my week to see them, but I don't see anything wrong with stopping by their day care to see them if I happen to be in the area. In addition, I didn't get to see them last weekend because you changed plans at the last minute."

None of what he said meant anything to her. Even the onlooking day-care workers were shocked by her behavior. She was unreasonable and ridiculous, so he didn't bother to argue with her. She got into her car and sped off without letting him kiss his children good-bye, and they burst out screaming when they were whisked away from him. As was typical of him during such moments, he entrusted the drama into the hands of God and remained calm while hoping that his battles were being fought for him by a higher power in whom he had absolute trust.

From then on, his visitation rights, although explicitly outlined in a court order, were subject to her whims and caprices. Seeing his children was nothing short of an emotional roller-coaster ride. Sometimes she would have the children ready in time and would even call to remind him to pick them up at the agreed-upon spot. Other times she would not answer the phone or respond to text messages for more than a week. And then she would let him pick up the children from her house or from her parents' just to follow that up with insinuations of sexual molestation of Jasmine over the weekend spent with him. She would claim to be taking her to the doctor for tests to prove the molestation, and he would never hear anything about it. The very next time she would tell nurses at the hospital where his son was hospitalized, "That's my husband," and he would remind her that he was not any such thing to her. Right after that, she would text him pictures of herself and her boyfriend kissing and making out, and she would include references to the guy's hefty genitals and athletic physique, to which he would respond, "I'm happy for you!" At times she would text him and call him all kinds of names in the cussing dictionary and would make him drive to Indianola in vain to pick up his kids, but she would go back to respecting the court order weeks later.

However, there was one area where she was consistently thoughtful: whenever she needed money other than the child support he was already paying, she would be incredibly nice to him. She would call him, text him, let him talk to his children on the phone, and even allow him to see and or pick them up earlier than scheduled. He could see right through it, but he just let her continue making a fool of herself.

Some of his friends advised him to take her to court for repeatedly violating the visitation order, while others suggested that he take the order to the police or to the sheriff whenever she didn't allow him to see his children, and they would storm her house and get the children from her by force. He agreed to do the former, but he vehemently turned down the latter approach. He thought that it was absolutely repugnant. It would traumatize any baby or toddler to be taken forcefully from his or her mother by uniformed officers. Apart from that, such a move could further backfire and cause the children to hate their father. So he resolved to continue exercising patience, resilience, and perseverance while trusting that God would handle his problems for him as long as he kept his hands clean.

Chapter Thirty

Financial Tsunami

Apart from the troubles with his ex-wife, Austin was ravaged by dire financial turmoil even though he was making more money than he had in Indianola. His income was just not enough to pay his bills, maintain his car, and take care of his basic needs. Paid leisure and relaxation were completely unaffordable. Some months he would ignore his knee-high stack of credit-card bills in order to pay his attorney's fees, which were also accruing interest on a daily basis, while at other times he would skip the mortgage payment and use the money to make minimum payments on his nine credit cards and to pay something on accumulating hospital bills, furniture notes, and personal loans from banks, credit unions, and individuals. He was submerged in debt, and the inundation was only getting worse.

Out of desperation, he reached out to people he believed were close friends for help. Some told him that they had their own problems, while others were willing to loan him money at terms that would bite deeper than those of loan sharks. One of his well-off friends, a former boss he had known for many years and had held in high regard, gave him the most ridiculous runaround when he asked him for a $200 loan. He told Austin that he needed his wife's permission to loan him the money that he had desperately driven all the way from Byram to Indianola to collect. But when Austin got to his home, the man said that he would take him to Planters Bank, where he would persuade a friend of his to loan him the money even though he knew that no bank would loan Austin a piece of paper out of their trash can because of his sunken credit. When they got to the bank, Austin's friend did not want to cosign for the loan when the banker said the borrower's credit was deplorable. After the failed mission to the bank, the so-called friend eventually gave him the money when he saw that it was almost midnight and Austin had to drive back home and go to work the next day. That kind of treatment from someone he respected made him vow to return the money as soon as he got paid four days later.

On April 15, 2011, he received a notice of intent to foreclose from the mortgage loan servicer, Bank of America. If he did not pay the three months past-due balance with all the fees and charges, a total of $5,425, within thirty days, his house would be foreclosed upon. He immediately sprang into action, knowing he had no one to count on but himself. He took his wedding ring, three guitars and amplifier, a Wii game console that he had bought for Jasmine and Jacob a week earlier, TV sets, and other household and clothing items to a pawnshop on I-55 in Jackson. He was given less than $600 for everything, which was worth thousands of dollars. He was still close to $5,000 short of his goal. Next, he checked out a payday advance location in Byram to ask for a loan, but they could only give him $600. He considered ignoring every other bill that month and surviving on only ramen noodles and water, but that would still leave him a couple of thousand short of what he needed to save the house that he had fought so hard to keep in the divorce battle. He lost his appetite and could not sleep at night. His students and colleagues noticed that he often seemed preoccupied, absent minded, and troubled.

With thirteen days left to the deadline, he found out about two programs that could help him keep his house. One was refinancing, but when he called to inquire about the conditions, he was told that he did not qualify for refinancing because his credit was shitty. The second was home affordability help, which Bank of America gave to qualifying homeowners. He submitted his application with all the one million and three required documents, but each time he called to check on the status of his application, he was kept on hold for hours and then told to send some more documents, most of which he had already sent with the application. And time was rapidly running out.

On the eve of the deadline, he drove to Indianola to see if his tenant could pay his rent early and even pay an advance on the next month's rent, but the lessee was of no help. That meant that the house would certainly go into foreclosure unless a miracle were to happen in the next twelve hours. As he left his rental property on French Road and made a left on the 448 to drive toward Highway 82, he saw a sign at a shopping plaza on his left that read Indianola Tower Loan. A voice in his head told him to turn in to the parking lot and go into the cash-advance business.

"Welcome to Tower Loan! How may I help you?" the lady behind the counter asked.

"Good evening! I would like to apply for a loan."

"How much would you like?"

"Two thousand dollars."

That was how much he would need to add to what he already had from pawning his valuables, skipping all his bills for that month, and getting a payday loan from the loan shark in Byram. The lady asked a few questions about his income and place of employment and then told him that he was approved for the $2,000 at an interest rate of 24 percent and a monthly payment of nearly $300. He was too excited about the approval to really care about the details in fine print.

"Thank you, Jesus!" he screamed, shook the loan officer's hand, and dashed out of the office as if he were afraid she could change her mind and rescind the loan approval.

The next day, the deadline, Austin purchased a certified check and mailed it to the Bank of America. He called to inform them that the check was on the way. That same day a notice was placed on his door for not paying his May rent on time, but he took it to the business office to speak to the manager.

She smiled and asked, "Why did you not tell me that you needed an extension?"

Antoine F. Gnintedem

"I didn't want to bother you. Give me a few days, and I'll take care of it. I've always paid my rent since I moved to this complex."

She approved his extension without hesitation.

He had slept with her a few times but had always resisted her demands for a full-blown, exclusive relationship. His very recent divorce was his go-to excuse. "The wounds are still too fresh," he would say. "Just give me some time to recover, and I'll be all yours." From then on, he was up front with the women he went out with. He had much bigger fish to fry than to be bothered with the strings of a serious relationship.

Chapter Thirty-One

Finding Another Way Out

On January 17, 2012, Austin had to take two grueling comprehensive exams consecutively, one for a specialist degree and the other for the doctoral degree in educational leadership that he was pursuing. He had found out earlier that week that he had already completed more than enough credit hours to qualify for a specialist degree that could enable him to become certified as a school administrator while he was finishing his doctorate. As a school administrator, he could earn more money to help with his continuously swelling debts. Taking both exams consecutively was going to be uniquely challenging physically and mentally, but he had been strengthened by other obstacles that he had already traversed in the valley of the shadow of death. He took the exams back to back from 8:00 a.m. to 10:45 p.m. A feat like that had never been attempted in the history of Delta State University, and both the dean of the college of education and the doctoral programs coordinator were very proud of him when he passed both comps at his first attempt with flying colors.

With his specialist degree in hand, he took the school-leadership licensure exam and obtained a very high score that guaranteed him certification in any state he wanted to be certified in. For a long time, he had contemplated moving to Tennessee, where the pay for educators, especially in Memphis, was about 25 percent higher than where he worked in Mississippi. That much higher, just next door, was too irresistible to not make a run for. Consequently, he applied for school-leadership jobs in Memphis and Nashville and waited eagerly for a reply. When he had not received any positive updates by the end of May, he concluded that it might not be a bad idea to pursue a teaching position in one of those cities. Once he had proved himself as a highly effective teacher, it would be less challenging to advance to his desired position(s), he thought.

On June 7, 2012, he caught his first break. He was invited to interview for a teaching job at Covington High School, forty-three miles outside Memphis. The principal scheduled the interview for the next day at 10:00 a.m., but she wasn't there when he got to the school. She had traveled to Nashville for a meeting that morning. Why did she have him drive for four hours all the way from Byram, Mississippi, if she knew that she was not going to be available? She could have at least called to cancel or reschedule the interview. When he called her to find out what to do, she asked him to come back the next day at the same time. What did she think he was? He was very angry.

As he left Covington High, he got another call to interview for an English opening in the same school district, at Brighton High School, a few miles away. He got there on time, at noon, but that principal too was busy. He was asked to sit in a waiting room. He waited for an hour and a half. Then a lady appeared and introduced herself as the assistant principal and said that she had been instructed by the principal to conduct the interview. The whole thing turned out to be an embarrassing joke. He could sense by the lack of seriousness attached to the interview that it was a waste of his time, but he still answered all ten questions thoughtfully and effectively. It was just his nature to take anything job related with the utmost seriousness. He left that building disappointed and frustrated, but something happened moments later to ease these feelings.

When he was a few miles out of Memphis on I-55, on his way back to Byram, the human-resource manager at Shelby County Schools called to find out if he would be interested in interviewing the next day for a dual (English and French) position at one of the district's high schools. He accepted the 9:00 a.m. appointment without hesitating. Memphis was where he really wanted to be. He had applied to the other districts in Tennessee only to avoid putting all his eggs in one basket.

The interview the next day with the principal of Bolton High School went extremely well. He was offered the job on the spot. He was going to be making $17,000 more than what he was making in Mississippi, even though the cost of living in Memphis was not dissimilar to what he was used to. The extra money would help him stem the financial tide that he had been drowning in for quite a while. He was also given a soccer-coaching position at the school, and it added more change to his pockets. For the first time in many years, he was truly hopeful. The somber, gray cloud that he thought had permanently blocked the sun over him was starting to dissipate. He thanked God for the immense blessing.

One other person who was equally excited about the job offer in Memphis was Karen, his girlfriend who lived there. To her it meant that she would not be driving to Byram anymore to see him. She even saw it as an opportunity to get even more. She was hoping that they could get married, or at least move in together, even though he had been clear about his lack of interest in marriage from the get-go a year earlier. She was going to be brutally disappointed. Austin was in a tough spot. Although he loved her, he didn't want to start anything that he did not want and that would send the wrong message.

Thus, to the great chagrin of Karen, he moved into an apartment in a gated community in Bartlett, twelve miles away from his school and thirteen miles from Memphis. She was inconsolable initially, but she progressively realized that she would lose him altogether if she didn't let the issue go completely.

Austin loved his job and was determined to do it outstandingly. He taught three classes of junior English and three French I courses. At the end of the first academic year, his students performed exceptionally well in the state end-of-course assessment, thereby making him a level-five teacher, the highest level a teacher could achieve in Tennessee. It denotes the highest level of teaching effectiveness, and being in this top tier brought him exposure and recognition. Another distinction for him at the end of that school year was his graduation from Delta State University with his second doctorate in educational leadership.

Consequently, he started his second year at Bolton with a red feather in his hat and with tremendous optimism. In the middle of the second semester, there was a vacancy for an assistant principal at his school, and he decided to apply for the highly contested position. After two rounds of interviews, he was one of the two finalists. In the end, the job was given to the other finalist, who had been with the district for more than a decade and already had experience in school leadership. In fact, she worked at the central office of the district and had facilitated a professional development session on his first day working for the school system.

This lady had captured Austin's attention and kept it during her presentation on that first day, but he didn't tell her because she was surrounded by other presenters all that day. However, he hoped to find out more information about her and to speak to her as soon as the opportunity presented itself. This came a month later when he, along with other new teachers in the district, had to attend another professional development session at the school board. Although he still didn't get a chance to speak to her at that workshop, he made sure that he left a lasting impression on her, as he would smile each time she looked in his direction or walked by him. It was definitely clear to her that she had an admirer.

As the assistant principal, she would be working with him. Fate had finally created the perfect opportunity for him to make his move. It was either then or never. Another thing that made the moment perfect was that his relationship with Karen was hanging by a thin thread that was weaker than a string on a spider's web. She had not completely given up on pressing him to get married to her or move in with her. One day, it rained so profusely in Memphis that her apartment complex got flooded. As a result, he allowed her to live in his apartment until hers was fixed, but three days into her stay with him, she got furious because he inquired about the progress of the work on her place. She wrathfully collected her belongings and stormed out. He didn't go after her. That pulled the curtains on their relationship.

Austin's second year ended even stronger than the previous one. The graduating class invited him to speak at their baccalaureate ceremony. He was nervous about the task because even though he had given speeches before, they had been mostly to much smaller crowds, and they had been mostly to groups that wanted to hear him talk about differences between African and American cultures. He knew that speaking to teenagers celebrating the end of their K–12 educational journey and going off to postsecondary opportunities would require an inspirational, motivating, hopeful, uplifting, moving, and captivating rhetorical piece. He gave it the attention and seriousness it deserved, and after two weeks of research and writing, he completed what he thought the audience of students, parents, family members, friends, faculty, staff, administrators, and other attendees would be pleased to hear. It read thus:

What's Your Excuse to Not Be Great?
A Speech Delivered by Dr. Austin Annenkeng at the
2014 Bolton High School Baccalaureate Ceremony

Let me begin by congratulating the entire class of 2014, especially the crème de la crème gathered here today. After twelve years of hard work and sometimes burning the midnight candle, you have earned your transition into the next and most crucial phase of your life. Congratulations on your outstanding achievement.

As you embark on the next phase of your academic journey, do not let anyone fool you that things are about to get easier. Many changes await you in the next few months. For instance, your education is not going to be free and mandatory anymore. Many of you have already earned thousands of dollars in scholarships to fund your way through undergrad. That is tremendously helpful. You are going to start paying for your books, food, transportation, and numerous other things that you previously had access to at school for free. Even more significant, unlike in the past twelve years when teachers gave you assignments and walked you through the process of completing them while repeatedly reminding you of the due dates, get ready to meet professors who will give you your course syllabus with your assignments and their respective due dates, and it will be your responsibility to have them done and submitted in time. And this is not even the full picture of the changes that lie ahead of you.

Nevertheless, I am not just absolutely convinced that you are going to rise to the challenge, but I am also certain that you will adapt easily to the changing circumstances because, by successfully completing IB, AP, honors, dual enrollment, and other pretty challenging courses in the past years, you have proven to be overwhelmingly resilient, dedicated, assiduous, persistent, and perseverant ladies and gentlemen.

Similarly, my conviction that you are going to do whatever it takes to be successful in undergrad and certainly beyond is strengthened by the fact that you understand it is your only reliable ticket to a meaningfully productive and contributing life. Again, are things going to be easy? No! Are the challenges ahead of you tougher than the ones that you have crushed thus far? Absolutely! However, as the famous author Joseph Marine states, "Challenges are what make life interesting and overcoming them is what makes life meaningful."

You have successfully completed all the courses that were required for graduation because you want to have an edge in your pursuit of a bright future. That glowing future will certainly be yours. After all, you live in the only country on the face of this planet where individuals who work hard, like you, can become anything they desire. Graduating seniors in other parts of the world, especially in Africa, where I was born and raised, do not have the kinds of guarantees that the United States has reserved for you.

After twelve years of paid elementary, middle, and high-school education, during which they have to buy their books and every other school supply, bring or buy food at school, and walk an average of twenty-five miles to and from school every day to attend classes in the most rudimentary of learning environments you can think of, your peers in Cameroon, Congo, Equatorial Guinea, Gabon, Chad, and Benin, just to name these, graduate into a postsecondary life of hopelessness; despair; and perpetual physical, emotional, and financial struggle. Unlike you, who are guaranteed a great career after college if you consistently work hard, the vast majority of your peers in these countries have nothing but uncertainty and misery awaiting them if they graduate from college. That is because getting a job in these countries, regardless of the type and level, does not depend on what you know and can do, but it depends on whom you know and how much money you have. You could be the valedictorian of your college class but never get a job for the rest of your life, while your classmate who failed every class and dropped out of college your sophomore year would get the best jobs in the country because he was born in the right family. This is one of the most sinister situations a human being can ever find himself or herself in. If one is born poor, one would spend one's entire life around people of similar circumstances and, consequently, one would have neither the connections nor the money that is crucial to getting a job in these countries.

That is why every day thousands of hopeless individuals are fleeing Africa and other parts of the globe and risking everything, some even swimming across massive bodies of water, and others trekking through jungles to seek even a remote shot at the life that you have in this uniquely blessed country. Every month I am called by the US Department of Justice and the US Department of Homeland Security to interpret at cases in immigration courts and immigration detention facilities around the United States. At each of these assignments, I see hundreds of people who would prefer to be held in a detention facility in the United States for months and even years, because it is better than conditions in their respective home countries. Think about this: a jail in the United States is better than freedom in someone's home country. I come back from these assignments heartbroken by what I saw and heard, and they make me appreciate what I have even more.

Therefore, class of 2014, go on to college and beyond knowing that you have everything you need to be hugely successful and that millions of graduating seniors around the world do not have even 1 percent of the resources and opportunities that are available to you in the United States. I hope that as you progress in life, you would open your eyes to the plight of the less fortunate around you and abroad and that your condition would inspire you to help proportionately to the means you have, or, as the great former US president, Teddy Roosevelt, put it, "Do what you can, where you are, with what you have."

As you get ready to begin the next and extremely important chapter of your life, let the words of the Greek philosopher Aristotle guide you as he says, "First have a definite, clear practical ideal; a goal, an objective. Second, have the necessary means to achieve your end; wisdom, money, materials, and methods. Third, adjust all your means to that end." Finally, and most importantly, let these words enshrined in the book of Matthew 7:7 always resonate in your mind: "Ask and it will be given to you; seek and you will find; knock and the door will be opened to you. For everyone who asks receives; he who seeks finds; and to him who knocks, the door will be opened."

Thank you very much!

He received a standing ovation when he finished. Many people walked up to him to congratulate him on a job well done. His bosses and colleagues also expressed their pride in him.

His supervisors and coworkers were given more reasons to be proud of him when state test scores came back a few days before the end of the academic year. His students did exceptionally well, and he was level five again. In recognition of his outstanding performance, he was named master teacher for the next school year. He would be teaching half-time and mentoring, training, coaching, and evaluating teachers the other 50 percent of his time. That promotion came with a pay raise and exposure. It was not the job that he wanted, but he was very thankful to God for the blessing. He was headed in the right direction. He was also looking forward to starting the next year with a good shot at the lady he had been admiring for a long time.

Chapter Thirty-Two

Now or Never

After strategizing for a long time, Austin finally made the move on September 15, 2013. He met the new assistant principal, Stacie Grant, in the parking lot as she was arriving on campus that morning. He complimented her on her fascinating beauty and asked if he could invite her to lunch or dinner the coming weekend. She didn't accept the invitation, but she didn't turn it down either. She said that she would think about it. Three weeks went by, and she still didn't say anything about it, even though they met at school almost daily.

Then, one beautiful fall afternoon in mid-October, she met him in the student parking lot, where they both had after-school duty, and asked him if he would like to go with her to a wine-tasting evening that her sorority, Alpha Kappa Alpha (AKA), was hosting at a local hotel. He told her that he would be honored to go, but, unfortunately, he had a prior commitment on the day of the event. However, he took her phone number so they could talk off campus. He called her a few days later and invited her to his apartment on Friday evening for wine and cheese. Her response to his second invitation was not ambiguous.

It started raining heavily two hours before the appointment, and Austin started doubting that she would be able to make it. Most people would not like to get out in such foul weather, especially when it involved going to see someone they barely knew on that person's home turf. But as abruptly as it started, the downpour ceased around 6:15 p.m., leaving forty-five minutes if she still wanted to make it.

She arrived twenty minutes late, and they spent almost two hours talking about a variety of subjects other than work. He couldn't believe that after two years of abstraction, imagination, dreaming, fascination, hesitation, desire, and obsession, the seeds of an amorous relationship with her were being sown right there on his couch. He inched closer to her and placed his hand on her right hand on the couch. She didn't resist, so he moved even closer and placed his left arm on her shoulder while leaning toward her. She replicated his moves, and they ended up in each other's arms. He could feel her warm, cotton-soft body underneath her short pink-and-white dress. They could hear each other's hearts pounding loudly. He held her tighter as their noses made contact and their lips locked. They were both ready for the lengthy kiss that ensued. He didn't want to appear predatory and cheap, so he stopped before things got hazy and fuzzy. They would have plenty of time in the future to do anything that they wanted. One thing seemed certain: they had deep, palpable interest and feelings for each other. Even after he told her that he was not hoping to get married or to have any more children in the future, she still was looking forward to a meaningful, romantic, passionate, and sustainable relationship with him.

Chapter Thirty-Three

Evolving Views

Austin and Stacie dated for three years without anyone at their school suspecting that they were in a relationship. They had decided to keep things that way until one of them found a job elsewhere. Thus, they went on dates out of town and hung out at each other's apartments. Their secret held tight for two years, but by the beginning of the third year, their feelings for each other were so strong that it blurred their vision occasionally and caused them to go to local restaurants, parks, and movies. On one occasion, a colleague of theirs and his wife saw them at the movies, but judging from their reaction, the colleague didn't think Austin and Stacie were a couple, especially as they did not act as if they even knew each other while at work.

The growing strength of their love for each other also transformed Austin psychologically. His long-held views about marriage and children were evolving progressively. He introduced her to his children after twenty-seven months of dating. He had avoided letting her meet them earlier because he didn't want either party to become attached, thereby complicating a breakup if the need for one came up. But by the second year, he was certain that it was the right thing to do. He also wanted to know what they thought about her and how she would perceive them.

The first time Stacie met Jacob and Jasmine was wonderful, Austin thought. It was at his apartment during one of his visitation weekends. An onlooker might have thought that the kids and their father's girlfriend knew each other quite well. They played games, chatted, sang, danced, cooked, drew, and did other fun things together. Stacie also took Jasmine shopping while Jacob hung out with his father at home. On Sunday evening, both of them drove to Jackson to return the kids to their mother. Her husband and she had moved there a few weeks after Austin left Byram in July 2012. On the way, Jasmine and Jacob played games with their new friend and made plans for their next meeting. Austin was very impressed and satisfied with the outcome and, as a result, he thought about stepping things up one notch.

On Valentine's Day 2015, he invited Stacie to accompany him to pick out the plan for a new house that he wanted to build a few blocks away from his apartment. After paying off all his credit-card debt and personal and payday loans in the three years since he had arrived in Tennessee, he became determined to stop paying for an apartment that was never going to be his even in a million years. He wanted her to help him select a plan for a single-family home because he had concluded that it would not be a bad thing if they ended up as husband and wife one day. If that were to happen, they would not need to look for another house, since she would have helped to pick a house in which she could see herself living very comfortably.

Any normal-thinking guy would want her for a spouse. She was not only extraordinarily attractive, but she was also very kind, ambitious, hardworking, smart, gentle, caring, fashion-conscious, neat, organized, supportive, deeply but sanely religious, and more. He knew these things about her after a few months of dating, but what really pushed him over the line was her treatment of his children. She saw them as hers, and she showed them as much love as she had for him. She was the type of woman a guy would proudly take home to his family.

She did have room for improvement in some areas, though. For instance, she couldn't save herself in the kitchen if her life depended on it. The previous Christmas, three of the presents that he gave her were some of the best cookbooks available on the market. They were like road maps to different types of appetizing cuisines. Additionally, he sometimes had the impression that he was competing with her sorority functions for her attention. But what actually worried him initially was her Pentecostal background (her parents were preachers), as it reminded him of his ex-wife, who had a similar background and whose parents were also preachers. The hypocrisy that he had witnessed daily for four years with his ex and her family left haunted him for a long time, and anything that remotely reminded him of it took him immediately to a bad place. However, she eventually proved herself to be unlike what he was afraid of. His fears were further assuaged when he eventually met her parents and found them to be very genuine, kind, welcoming, nonjudgmental, friendly, and supportive.

Stacie was not perfect, but who was? He was not looking for perfection. She was fully aware of her wrinkles and was making committed, sustained efforts toward smoothening them. That was all that mattered to him.

He sought her input at every stage of the construction of the house. When he traveled home to Cameroon to see his family a few months into the project, he put her in charge of it. The house was completed in September 2015, and he asked her if she would mind moving in with him. She accepted despite the concerns of her parents. Even though they liked Austin a lot, they frowned on the idea of their only child living with her boyfriend without being married to him.

Chapter Thirty-Four

Second Time's a Charm

Austin didn't keep Stacie's parents worried about their daughter cohabiting with him for too long. In fact, on February 27, 2016, he asked the most consequential question of their relationship with a beautiful emerald-cut diamond ring, and she agreed to be united with him forever, for better and for worse. Within days they scheduled their wedding for December 17 of the same year and immediately started planning.

The preparations were very intense and, at times, caused friction between the two lovebirds. For example, she was very particular about certain things she wanted to have and do at the church ceremony and at the reception, although those minute details, such as sticking letters under their shoes to spell out "I do," were just taking too much time and energy that could be used elsewhere. He told her that she could have all of those things and even more if she would spare him the headache of planning for them. Compromise was thus struck.

Their wedding guests came from around the United States and from other countries. Austin's immediate family members flew in from Cameroon and England. His mother arrived one month ahead in order to spend time with her grandchildren, whom she had never met. They were very excited to finally meet her. They had spoken to her regularly on the phone and via Skype, but that was not as thrilling as meeting her. The kids were also delighted to be included in the wedding as flower girl and ring bearer, but that pleasure was almost ruined when their mother insisted that she and her husband had to accompany them to the wedding.

Who desires to be at the wedding of his or her ex-spouse? That was a crazy idea, and neither Austin nor Stacie liked it.

On December 14, 2016, Austin, Stacie, and her soon-to-be mother-in-law left for Jackson for Jasmine's birthday celebration at a trampoline park. They also hoped to dissuade his ex from coming to their wedding, but they were certain that it would just lead to her preventing the children from participating in the wedding regardless of the fact that such a thing would break their little hearts. After talking about the issue for two hours on their way to the birthday celebration, they concluded that if the kids' mother and stepfather wanted to make fools of themselves in front of hundreds of strangers by coming to the wedding, they would not stop them. They didn't want anyone to ruin Jacob and Jasmine's burning desire to be in the festivities.

The birthday celebration was a remarkable success. Austin had never seen Jasmine as happy as she was that afternoon. She acted as if a longtime dream of hers had finally come true. She was surrounded by the people she loved and who loved her doubly, including her mother and father, stepfather, soon-to-be stepmother, grandmother from Cameroon, sister, brothers, friends, classmates, cousins, and some of her friends' parents. The birthday celebration was just a precursor of the bigger celebration that she couldn't wait to be a part of.

Three days later, Austin and Stacie tied the knot in an elaborate ceremony that was officiated by her father, Pastor/Mayor Peter Grant, at his newly constructed church in the bride's hometown of Louisville, Mississippi. The church was filled with family, friends, and colleagues. Apart from Austin's sister Marie, her husband, and their two children, who had flown in from London, a dozen of the groom's friends also came in from distant parts of the United States. It was a reunion of good friends who had not seen one another in years. Six of them were the groomsmen. The latter along with the elated ring bearer, Jacob, were dressed in black suit, shoes, string tie, and white shirt, while the groom donned a gray suit, white shirt, black shoes, and black bow tie. The six bridesmaids and three flower girls looked radiant in their black dresses, black shoes, and diamond jewelry. The bouquets and baskets, respectively, that they carried adorned their outfits and enhanced the beauty of the event. The bride outshone everyone in her magnificent white dress with a long train. She also wore a diamond tiara, earrings, bracelets, and white high-heel shoes. She was phenomenally gorgeous!

Meanwhile, the church was beautifully decorated with meticulous attention. The choir and other guest musicians played both familiar and specially composed tunes that electrified the room. The excitement in the building could be seen even by the blind, and even Kimberly, her husband, and her two older kids seemed to be genuinely happy for the newlyweds.

The reception, which followed the church ceremony, was not any less meticulously organized. The menu featured cuisines and drinks from around the world, all prepared by chefs and experts hired for the occasion. There was more than enough to eat and drink. Austin had no use for the collection of Cameroonian and Congolese music that he had prepared because the DJ who was hired surprised them with his significant repertoire of tunes from these and other parts of the world. The reception lasted beyond 2:00 a.m., something unusual for people in the city. Even professed nondrinkers of alcohol were spotted downing beer, wine, champagne, whiskey, and cocktails.

Austin and Stacie did not leave for their honeymoon that night, according to tradition, because they had scheduled a romantic getaway to Key West, Florida, from December 28 to January 4. They wanted to give the scores of guests who were staying at their residence time to catch their respective return flights. The last person to leave was his mother, on December 27.

Chapter Thirty-Five

Familiar Foe Returns

A horrendous surprise was waiting for the newlyweds when they returned to their home in Bartlett, Tennessee, the evening after the best day of their life. It was a letter from the Mississippi Department of Human Services informing the father of Jacob and Jasmine that, at the request of the custodial parent, Kimberly, a review of his income was to begin in two weeks in order to decide the amount by which his child-support payments would be increased. He was being ordered to submit documentation of all his sources of income immediately, or the state would obtain it through other means. He was stunned that they were asking him for documents that were already in the possession of DHS, since his monthly child-support payments were automatically taken from his paycheck every two weeks at the request of the state of Mississippi.

"She's just looking to get more money now that we're married, honey," Stacie said.

"I know, and that doesn't surprise me. But why today, though? That woman is incredibly evil. She launched this the day before we all met at Jasmine's birthday party to ensure that I would receive the letter from the DHS the day before or, at the latest, the day after the wedding," Austin said.

"That is diabolical! I can't believe she and her husband had the audacity to act so nice and friendly at the birthday celebration and then pretend to be genuinely happy for us on our wedding day, knowing that they had triggered something to torpedo our joy," Stacie said angrily.

To say the letter was a huge damper on the wedding celebration would be an understatement. It was a major distraction from everything that they had planned to do upon their return home. He stayed up until 5:12 a.m. the next day. He stared at the ceiling in the dark and plunged into an unprecedented and unparalleled depth of pensiveness. He went back to his birth and childhood in a remote and terribly rural part of Cameroon, with all its abject poverty, misery, corruption, disease, nepotism, xenophobia, and so on sternly staring at him every day. He unlocked the memories of his teenage and college days, all full of dreams and hopes for things that he wanted to accomplish to improve the living conditions of his parents, siblings, and community. He saw how each time he took a step forward toward accomplishing these dreams, an obstacle appeared out of nowhere to cause them to be deferred. The constant and suffocating misery, systemic corruption, rampant disease, chronic poverty, stinging debt, and frequent deaths had squeezed him out of Cameroon in search of alternative ways of achieving his goals. But even seventeen thousand miles away in the United States, those things reappeared at every corner, although in different robes. Each time he made progress, something would come up, at times out of his own stupidity, to set him back a few steps. "Why can't I just stay on the path to progress and success, a track without bumps and roadblocks? Is that too much to ask from God? Have I and my family been cursed?" he wondered out loud, not enough to wake his wife sleeping next to him.

He was working very hard and using very honest and legitimate means to bring joy and a better life to his family and community, but it seemed that the harder he worked and the more progress he made, the more challenges appeared, far beyond his control, making his dream absolutely elusive. Some of the challenges would leave a very bitter taste in his mouth, one so strong that he could still taste it even during periods of remarkable success.

"Is life just a cycle of sadness and anxiety preceding success and happiness over and over? How can one make the latter overwhelm and overshadow the former? How can one sustain and maintain happiness or at least make it last significantly longer than sorrow?" he asked. By that time his pillow was fully soaked. He knocked it off the bed. He concluded just before dawn that it was time to act drastically. It was time to make a commitment to be happy no matter what happened. He needed to start making solidly grounded efforts to implement some things that he had previously believed were easier said than done.

At some point during his battles with his ex-wife, his friend and former boss, Mr. Brown, had told him, "Don't worry about things you can't control." Problems seemed to be a part of life, and if he was going to worry about them, he might as well be making arrangements to be worried and sad for the rest of his life, because they would not stop coming at him in all shapes, sizes, colors, and so on, regardless of his location.

He thought about what his late father used to say in the face of the numerous hurdles that he had surmounted in his life. He would always say, in Pidgin English, "That one na something?" and "Man no fit kill yi self." His dad always downplayed the problems that befell him, regardless of how minute or how massive they were, such as the diabetes and high blood pressure that plagued him for decades and eventually choked the life out of him. He valiantly confronted each of his obstacles without standing down, always with that contagious smile on his face. Austin decided to pull that page out of his father's playbook to use as a road map to the sustained happiness that he so desperately wanted. What had made his father so happy all the time was a quality that was inherent and innate. It was a character trait that had been in him from birth. It was reinforced and perfected by each obstacle that he faced in his sixty-seven years on earth. Nothing in life could have taken it away from him. He had come with it and had left with it. That intrinsic motivation to be happy and to not let extrinsic variables cloud his sun was what Austin wanted. According to psychologists such as Abraham Maslow, all human beings possess it. They just need to reach deep down in themselves and pull it out in order to use it to reach and live to their full potential and be happy.

Austin came out of that deep and prolonged pensive state with a firm and unyielding commitment to living a happy life, regardless of the obstacles that were certainly ahead of him as long as he was one of the billion people on earth. He took stock of the bountiful blessings that God had bestowed on him in thirty-nine years. In fact, he realized that there weren't enough digits on any calculator to count the number of ways that the Lord had been good to him. He resolved that henceforth he would focus on those blessings and look for the silver lining in every obstacle that he came across. He would only look at life with a glass-half-full mind-set.

When he woke up late that morning, he contacted an attorney in Jackson and forwarded her the letter from the DHS. After two months of submitting additional information and documentation to the DHS through his lawyer, he received a letter from the former stating that there wasn't enough evidence found to support an increase in child support at that time.

"God is good, all the time," he said.

About the Author

Antoine F. Gnintedem is a renowned educator both in the United States and across the world. As a linguistic consultant, he has worked for the Department of Defense, the Department of Justice, and the Department of Homeland Security. In addition, he has served as an educational assessment expert for leading national and international testing companies. His academic achievements include a PhD in English language and literature and another doctorate in educational leadership.

Made in the USA
Lexington, KY
30 January 2018